To my readers for sharing the love

Spin Me Round

The Complete Collection

By
Elle Carmichael

Editing by SG Thomas and Swish Design and Editing
Cover by Najla Qamber Designs

Book Layout © 2017 BookDesignTemplates.com

Spin me Round/ Elle Carmichael. -- 1st ed.
ISBN 978-0-6480249-5-8

Spin Me Round

The Complete Collection

garnet

hen the room darkens I stir from my sleep, knowing the sun has set. I keep the hours of a vampire because I like to party hard, and last night was a killer. My whole body screams as though I'd thrown myself in front of truck speeding along the freeway.

Move your butt, Garnet, my subconscious demands.

Forcing my naked ass out of my bed, I head for the shower to soothe my aching body. Before I make it, I hear muffled voices coming from the kitchen. I head toward the sound and hurl open the door.

Fuck.

I didn't expect my girl's mother to be paying a surprise visit. "Morning, Missus Van Heusen," I say, leaning against the doorframe. My polite greeting falls flat as her brow pinches and her gaze lowers, surveying me.

Her mouth falls open. "It's the evening," she says in contempt before turning away and scooping her handbag from the table. "That's my cue to leave." She leans and kisses Lena on the cheek. "Please visit more. Redondo Beach is not that far away, and then I wouldn't need to experience any more insufferable visits here."

"You mean, surprise unannounced visits," I grumble.

Lena shoots me a look before standing to walk her mother to the door. "I'm happy, Mom," she says in her quiet tone. "I want you to remember that."

The front door slams, cutting off the remainder of the conversation.

"Whatever." I turn and head toward the shower. From my bedroom window I have an aerial view of Lena and Missus Van Heusen walking across the lawns of the apartment complex. I watch Missus V hug her daughter tightly as though she needs saving.

Fuck off.

In the shower I lather mango-scented gel across my shoulders, then down and over my tits. I close my eyes, remembering how Lena's mouth caressed my breasts before we headed out last night. Basically, I don't recall much after the ABC shots—Absinthe, Bacardi 151, and Chartreuse are potent on their own, but together they can fuck a girl up good. Figures why I can't remember much after we got home.

All I know is that I could use some of her loving now. Before I finish rinsing the conditioner from my hair, Lena steps into the bathroom. I smile at her and open the glass door invitingly.

She folds her arms across her chest and leans back against the basin. "You could've spared Mom the shock of seeing you naked," she says in her gentle voice.

Wiping water from my eyes, I say, "I didn't know she was here." Hell, if I'd known, I'd have gladly stayed curled up in bed rather than face the witch.

"Yet you struck a pose in the doorway, ensuring every one of your tattoos was on display."

"You're worried about her seeing my tattoos?" I ask incredulously. Then I smile. I enjoy shocking her mother.

"Not all of them." She half-smiles at me.

"You mean, this one?" I point to the ruby-colored rose above my clit, the long stem finishing below my navel.

Lena tilts her head at me.

"My sleeve? Or maybe these." I caress my own breasts and fondle the piercings. "I know *you* like these," I tease. When she doesn't say anything, I jerk my head. "C'mon, Lena, jump in here with me."

Lena pushes off the basin. Just when I think she's about to accept my invitation, she pulls open the bathroom door. "No, Gar. We're already late. Dinner at Xavier's started an hour ago."

Hell.

Lena and Xavier are my family. Not the blood type because my parents fucking suck. Before my heart fractures at the memory of my pathetic upbringing, I open my legs wider and locate the spot that gives me pleasure and help me to forget.

I'm going to enjoy the night with my friends, even more so than last night because I don't have a gig.

Tonight is going to be massive.

garnet

The Rox nightclub has pulled in a fair crowd. The DJ, Claire Knight, is a friend, and I'm glad she's getting to spin here on my nights off.

"Another round?" I shout at Xavier, who is sitting across from me at a round table in the VIP area. He gives me the thumbs up before turning back to some chick chatting him up.

Leaning down I kiss Lena, enticing her to open her mouth wider by caressing her plump lips. "And a shot for you?" I whisper on her lips.

"Of course." She smiles, and those gorgeous dimples are on display.

Making my way to the bar, people clear a path like I'm parting the Red Sea. Hell, they better. I own this fucking club since I provide the dance vibes four nights a week. Everyone wants on my door list.

"Four ABC shots," I shout at Cohen behind the bar. I hold up my fingers in case he doesn't hear me over the music. I'd better get one for the chick who has wormed her way into our table. "And don't skimp. I don't want any cheap shit. Wait. Make it eight." I decide to make it a double round.

"ABC? Not you're usual style," he says.

"Yeah, well, tonight it is." And last night. Can't a girl get hammered and not be judged? I roll my eyes and turn when a warm body melts into my right side. I glance up to the most amazing green eyes—for a guy—and step away. He nudges his shoulder closer to me when some jerk pushes toward the bar on his other side.

"Garnet."

Christ, my name rolls off his tongue like melted caramel. I shrug one shoulder at him. "Most people know my name." I'm staring back at him. He's familiar. The buzz cut...and those eyes. I know those eyes. He's not smiling. A muscle ticks in his angular jaw, and it's fucking sexy—if I were into him.

"That they do. And most know mine. Can I buy you a drink?"

In perfect timing Cohen returns with a tray of shots.

I dismiss hot guy with a wink. "Got it covered, but thanks for the offer."

I pick up the tray and before I move, he leans in, his lips brushing my ear. "You haven't even heard what I'm offering. And it's not for public viewing."

I'm frozen to the spot. Is he for fucking real? "Clearly, you don't know anything about me."

"On the contrary. I know quite a lot about you, Gar." I jerk when he calls me the pet name used only by my close friends. He sweeps in and his lips brush my neck. My whole body tingles. "And I'd like to see that tattoo on your pussy."

Well, shit. He *does* know a lot about me. "Fuck off." I shove the tray into his chest, and the shot glasses spill over him before smashing to the ground.

He chuckles low but there's no humor in his tone. Rather, I get the feeling I've just upped the stakes. His gaze drills into me. What I see behind his eyes is startling—a look I struggle to make sense of, but it's full of intent, desire, and control. The latter has me taking a step back... only a small step... because I don't like to back down. The cool control he exudes is now consuming me, and judging by his smug expression, that's exactly what he intends.

One hand swipes his chest before he lowers his gaze to assess the damage. It's then that I see his inked sleeve, the colors mesmerizing me. I'm familiar with the art— the eagle wings, gentle swirls leading to a rose, and a beautiful girl's face.

"Where do you live?"

"What?" I snap.

"Where do you live? I need an address where I can drop my shirt so you can have it dry-cleaned." My eyes fixate on his broad chest, specifically the pectoral muscles expanding the blue material as if it were spandex.

"Jesus, Garnet," Cohen whines. "Billy, move your ass and clean up Garnet's mess."

I glare at him. "It's this asshole's fault. Christ, give me another round, would ya, Cohen?" I turn away from those gorgeous green eyes, knowing I should know his name but I've lost all common sense.

"What'd ya do to her, Wes?" Cohen throws a cloth at him, but in a fast catch-and-release, it lands back in Cohen's hands.

My eyes round at his quick reflexes.

"Forget it, Cohen." Wes' fingers move to his buttons. Both hands are inked. One has the word *FLY* written across his three fingers. The other has *Veni Vidi Vici* lengthways on the inside of his wrist. I watch curiously as he peels his shirt down his arms to reveal a tribal pattern on his shoulder without the inked sleeve and the tattooed sculpted pecs I'd imagined. I'm ogling the words on his chest—*With Pain Comes Strength*—when he says, "Gar here is going to wash my shirt." Then he shoves said shirt into my hands.

I drag my gaze from his muscles. "The hell I am." Billy is by my feet cleaning up the mess around me. I push the shirt back at Wes before Cohen hands me another tray of shots. I immediately down two of the shots. My eyes clench shut when the burn travels down the back of my throat, and I'm quickly reminded what I was originally doing—getting wasted. When I open my eyes, Wes is watching me.

"What? Can't a girl get fucked up without an audience?"

"It's not the getting fucked up I'm opposed to. But I'm sure I could fuck you up...better."

Realizing some heads have turned my way, I play it cool. Plus, it's not his words I find offensive, but his lack of respect. He seems to know so much about me, and therefore I assume he knows I'm with someone. I lean in closer. "But you'll never know 'cause I don't dig dicks."

"Well, mine wouldn't object to watching you make out with your pretty partner." I narrow my eyes at him, then open my mouth to slay him with my tongue. Beating me to it, he adds, "Although I'd bet ten grand you'll be tasting my dick within a week."

"Cohen, can you kick this fucker outta here?" I say, almost begging.

"No, Garnet. Even you don't have that sort of weight to throw around."

"Guess the club wants my money." Wes smirks at me. "I'll send you my laundry bill, *Gar*."

"You'll be wasting your precious time."

"Guess you haven't read the papers. I have a lot of time to waste."

"Whatever, asshole." I push past him and head to the table where Lena and Xavier are waiting.

"What took you so long?" Lena takes the tray from my hands.

I wipe my sticky fingers over my jeans. "Some douchebag knocked over the first tray.

Do you know him?" I nod in Wes' direction. "Wes something or other."

"Wesley Black."

Christ, Lena almost orgasms saying his name. "Who?" I stare at Lena, a touch jealous.

"The NFL player. Oh, come on, Gar. Don't pretend you don't know him."

"I've heard something about him." Not that I take any notice of sports. "He apparently knows me."

"Everyone knows you," Xavier says in a tone that should make me proud. "The only thing missing in this club tonight is you rockin' it with your vibes."

I smile at Xavier, but my thoughts are still on Wes and why he tried to hook up with me, knowing I'm with Lena. Hell, I was bisexual once but I haven't been with a guy for five years. "So what's his story?"

"Bad boy fallen from grace because of drugs. He's made a shitload of money playing football, but he was recently given the boot. Surely you read about it online?"

"Drugs?"

Lena straightens. "Yeah. Cocaine." I stare at her and try to understand the expression on her face. Is she dismissing the fact that he was caught using but it doesn't matter because he's like some friggin' god, or the cocaine itself isn't a problem?

My girl doesn't mind cocaine. Me, I kicked that pleasure out the door years ago. I now prefer to get high from my music. Don't get me wrong, I'm no fucking saint. I can get drunk with the best of them, but I need all the sleep I can get with the hours I keep, and cocaine—the bitch from hell—is not about sleep.

I laugh once, wondering how many players do cocaine and don't get caught. "Unlucky bastard."

"The league is trying to clean up its act," Lena says, dismissing me. "You wouldn't understand because you don't follow football."

Grinning, I pull Lena onto my lap and kiss her cheek. She's adorable when she's frustrated. I look absently into the crowd and find Wes on the other side of the room. A few girls are gathered around him, but he's leaning against the wall with his eyes in my direction, his wet shirt clinging to his chest.

My hand lands on Lena's thigh and I knead her flesh, moving slowly higher. I'm half concentrating on her, half on Wes. I nuzzle Lena's neck while he stares at me. I trail my tongue along Lena's skin, feeling her quiver in my arms. He's watching me, watching him. He folds his arms and nods, egging me on. And damn if it's not turning *me* on.

Fuck! What the hell is wrong with me?

3

garnet

The following afternoon I wake with another headache from hell.

Lena creeps into the room.

"Oh, you're awake," she whispers.

"Yeah, baby."

"You have a ton of emails, and more packages have arrived. Can I open them?"

I chuckle lightly, trying not to make much sound. "Sure," I say as I reach for my head. "Can you bring me some water and aspirin?"

After Lena hands me a bottle, I throw two tablets to the back of my throat. I reach for the water and guzzle it down. Lena has opened the first box and squeals when she sees that her favorite designer has sent me half a dozen pieces. There's a benefit to being a popular female DJ. Fashion companies want their label on my back, especially when I have two hundred thousand Twitter followers. And even more on Instagram and Facebook.

Lena smells of mango so I know she's already showered and probably cleaned up the place too. Her mom has trained her well. Mine was an alcoholic so I moved out when I was sixteen. My mom hated her life and never wanted to be a single mom. She never told me who my father was. Anyway, I wasn't going to let her ruin my life as well as her own.

"How do I look?" Lena twirls in front of me wearing a backless floral shirt.

"Fucking sexy." I sit up and admire her olive skin.

She throws a pair of tiny pinstriped shorts at me. "These are yours. My legs are too fat for those."

"Bull-fucking-shit." I hate it when she bitches about herself. We've lived together two years and been together for three. Not once have I considered her body less than perfect.

"Well, I'm leaving this beauty on because we *are* going out for coffee."

"Pity the back isn't the front." I throw back the covers. Lena pauses, her eyes perusing my body. She steps to me and circles her finger around my nipple, tugging gently on the nipple ring.

"You want people to see my tits?"

My hand slips under the material and finds her nipple already peaking. I no longer give a shit about the top. "Take it off."

"Coffee first," she says. But her tone gives her mood away.

My fingers wrap around her wrist and I tug gently until her face is a mere inch from mine. "I love you," I whisper.

Lena moans against my lips. Sitting up, she yanks her top over her head and discards it on the floor. Then she shimmies out of her skirt— no panties. I give my dirty girl a wry smile. Making room for her next to me, I kick the sheets to the end of the bed. She slithers in beside me and her hands find my breasts, kneading small circles and building to larger ones. A satisfied noise escapes me when her mouth captures my nipple, and her tongue latches and sucks the piercing.

My boobs are my weakness. One touch and my legs open like magic. Maybe it's because I was a skinny kid with no curves because I was always starving. But although my mother wasn't good for much, I thanked the universe she gave me her genes and when I turned fourteen—voila!

Breasts.

My tits appear even bigger because of my small frame and they get plenty of attention. I've even used them to my advantage over the years. Hey, I did what I had to do to get where I am today.

No regrets.

Lena's tongue helps me to forget my thoughts. I arch my back, my legs opening wider. She pushes her fingers inside of me and finds the spot, teasing and rubbing, and I moan.

Her soft lips find mine. Tongues clash. Her hands keep busy, one hand inside of me and the other caressing my breast. Moving to my side, I switch my position so I find her clit with my fingers. I work the magic, knowing what she likes...what I like. Then I edge my fingers inside her and she gasps. Her pussy is like an oven around my fingers and so fucking wet. I push the third finger inside of her and she writhes next to me.

Lena bites my lower lip as she pulls away, her hand reaching into the bedside drawer. Reaching for the lube, I squirt it over the dildo she's holding. Lena sits to my side and watches as she guides the bulb-shaped end inside of me, rubbing my clit simultaneously. I groan, relishing the pleasure shooting into my abdomen. Lena positions herself on top and slides down on the other end. The double dildo is my favorite toy. I hold the base securely inside of me while Lena bounces on top. The action vibrates the dildo against my G-spot, sending me into a spiral of joy.

It's the *more* I need.

Our hips compose the rhythm. We come over and over and our screams echo around the room. Like a blanket of warmth, Lena falls forward and her dark hair falls around her face. Leaning up, I take her breast into my mouth and suck her nipple, my tongue swirling around the pebble.

"Garnet," she murmurs. The velvet sound strikes the perfect note. I tip her to the side and gently pull the dildo out and toss it aside. Scrambling to my knees, I place my hands on her thighs and open her legs so she is baring herself to me. I smile at her before dipping my head and sucking hard on her clit. She screams out, and her legs stretch wide as I push my tongue inside of her.

"That's it, baby," I murmur. "Let it all go."

My thumb presses on her clit while my tongue flicks and tastes her.

"Gar," she says, sounding breathless.

I smile and peer over her mound to see her satisfied expression. I blow gently on her wet labia, the cool air brushing over her warm, wet pussy, causing her to inhale sharply. I crawl up beside her and grin when she finally smiles back. Seeing her completed sated is so gratifying. I flop next to her and cup my arm around her waist, happy to lie there silently with her until she floats back to earth.

⁓

"How long will you be gone?" Lena's smile disappears after reading my emails and hearing how many music festivals I'm scheduled to attend around the country.

"I'll try and get home in between concerts." I kiss her cheek. I hate flying, but for Lena I'll do anything. "It's a good thing you took the manager position at Clique." Lena has worked at the fashion boutique for five years and was recently promoted while the owner is vacationing in Europe.

"The longer hours will keep me occupied." She forces a smile.

"You can come with me," I say. "Sit with me on the plane and keep my mind off... crashing."

Lena gently places her hand on my cheek. "You'll be fine and you know I can't take time off work. I've committed to working six days a week for the next eight weeks."

Realization hits me how long we'll be apart. "Then I'll definitely try and make a trip home, baby." Caressing her arm, I look into her blue eyes. "But I have to go. It's good money."

Lena exhales, resigned. "I know."

Scrolling through my emails, I line up the dates. Thirteen concerts in as many cities. I'll be so fucking tired over the next month I'll be shit company even when I'm home. "There's two more weeks before I leave, so no moping. Get dressed. We've missed coffee, so we'll go out for dinner."

After slipping on my ripped black jeans, I dress in a denim shirt, unbuttoned with a white tank top underneath. Using the straightener, my favorite tool, I style my hair, making sure to abolish any kinks. Lena changes into a short, tight-fitting black dress that accentuates her tits.

I roll a joint and share it with her. We laugh about the weekend and hate knowing it's coming to an end. But with Lena, watching her laugh as though I'm her world and knowing she finds me fucking interesting... well, at this moment, life is fucking great.

The Thai restaurant we frequent is only a few blocks away. We walk with our arms around each other, swaying across the pavement until we reach the front door of the restaurant.

"Lena and Garnet, welcome." Lim, the owner, nods at us. "I no see for a while."

"Been busy, Lim," I shoot over my shoulder.

"You making music?"

Stopping, and not sure how to answer him, I shrug. "Trying to." I get embarrassed talking about my success to people I'm not close to.

We order the usual chicken stir-fry, then I head to the restrooms. I've always liked the restaurant's black and red décor. Admiring the unusual artwork on the walls, my gaze finds a colorful Chinese dragon. It's the same art as the tattoo I've been contemplating. The five-clawed dragon is the symbol of power, strength, and good luck. It represents the yang in a relationship. Light and dark, life balance, and all that. But sometimes I wonder if Lena and I are truly opposites who complement each other, or whether we are connected by fate. Or maybe it's convenience. It's something I don't want to con-

sider as it only unlocks my dark thoughts so I block it out—it's what I do best.

I stroll further into the foyer, continuing to take in each painting, when a strong hand wraps around my wrist, halting me.

"Gar. Fancy seeing you here," Wes drawls.

Talk about dark shadows... "You fucking stalking me?"

"Do you want me to stalk you?"

I wrench my hand from his and glance over my shoulder toward my table where Lena is seated. "What I want is for you to stay away from me."

Wes gives me a satisfied smile. "You're afraid."

"Of you? Go fuck yourself."

"Of being with me." He leans in to whisper in my ear and the anticipation of his breath caressing my skin sends goose bumps all over me. "Because you know I can give you the best sex you've ever had. And now you're shaking like a fucking princess."

I step back and glare at him. "You know nothing of what I like." I spin away and head to the restrooms.

"You want to make a bet?"

I throw him a look over my shoulder. "You want to lose again? You lost the last bet."

He smiles as if he knows something I don't. "The week's not up yet."

My skin reacts like spiders are crawling over me. Inside the restroom, I wash my hands and dampen the back of my neck. I can't fathom why he's hell-bent on getting me into bed. He knows I'm in a relationship with Lena, yet he doesn't care.

Asshole

I pull out my phone and Google 'Wesley Black.' Immediately, my screen fills with football images and news reports on his drug arrests. Call it instinct or whatever, but I trust my gut and something tells me to steer clear of him.

I don't mention the encounter to Lena when I return to the table. As I'm almost finishing my meal, I look up, directly into Wes' piercing stare. Holy shit, he's eye-fucking me in a restaurant. I narrow my eyes at him, but it does nothing to break his gaze.

"Are you okay?" Lena reaches out and touches my hand.

"Yeah." I smile at her, but my attention shoots back to Wes. He crosses his arms and

leans forward on the table as though he's waiting for a show.

I'm not falling for it. I pick up Lena's hand and kiss her fingers. "I'm tired. Do you want to get outta here?"

"Sure, baby." She lets go of my hand then finishes her noodles. My gaze flickers to Wes, but a male friend has arrived and he's now blocking my view. My shoulders relax a little. It's enough for me to finish eating my noodles.

It's a beautiful mild, summer night so Lena and I walk home along the beach, and I feel a sense of contentment. There's plenty of activity happening on Venice Beach at night; it's one of my favorite places in the world. A place where I fit. Like an irregular shape fitting perfectly in a complex jigsaw puzzle.

"Mom wants me to move back home," Lena blurts out.

Her declaration kills the moment. "Hasn't she always? I mean, I *am* the devil."

"Don't talk like that." She squeezes my hand. "She thinks I can save more money living at home so I can eventually buy my own house."

"Did you tell her you don't pay much living with me?" Christ, what does the woman want? I own my apartment in a high-class area, and the only thing Lena pays for is half the food. "You could be saving money by living with me."

"I don't. I spend most of it partying. I'm starting to understand what Mom's saying."

"So, what are you asking...you want my permission to move out?"

Lena shakes her head. "No, of course not." Her brown hair falls forward, shielding her face. "I thought I'd move home while you're away. I won't be as lonely and it will make Mom happy."

I don't say anything at first. I'm pissed off—majorly. "Can't she accept you're happy and she doesn't need to *save* you?"

"After five weeks of staying with her, I hope I can convince her of that."

I nod. "And what about when I come home?"

"I'll come home too. I'm not telling you this to make you upset. I think it's a win-win for both of us."

"Especially your mother." I turn away and focus on the ocean shimmering under the moonlight.

Her hand squeezes mine and I prepare myself for what she's going to say next. "I know you didn't have a relationship with your mom, but I do. And I want to keep it that way."

"I respect that. Why can't she fucking respect us?"

Lena shrugs. "Give her time."

It's been three years...how much more time does she need?

4

garnet

aising my fist in the air, I scream, "Are you ready, Philadelphia? Let's rock this shit."

The crowd roars as I punch the air in a steady rhythm to the beat of my vibes. Seven stages are set up around the huge grounds, yet it appears most of the fans are in front of my stage.

Fucking yeah.

Heads bob, bodies bounce, and fists pump when I crank the volume. This is the world where I fit in, and everyone thinks I'm a fricken star. It's my addiction...my sanity. The beast within me feeds off their mood. I adjust my headphones, raise the bass, then punch the air harder.

"Show me your fucking love, Philly."

Another roar and I smile, pointing my finger at the crowd, catching the briefest glimpse because now the lights blind me. Neon lights dart across the masses in a crisscross action, making me dizzy. It's like processing a light seizure, the excitement rolling off the crowd in waves.

Raising my arm, I indicate they're numero uno. My body moves to a will of its own, bouncing to the beat. I throw my head back and smile to the heavens. I'm in my element with the stage lights blaring down on me.

Xavier stands to my left on the side of the stage. My ever-reliable manager. He gives me the thumbs up. Then my gaze settles on the tall, athletic guy in a suit beside him. At first I notice the buzz cut, but then I'm caught in those fucking green eyes.

What the hell is he doing here? Dressed in a fucking suit!

Wes shoots me an easy smile. I glare at him for a few seconds before turning back to my audience. This is my time to shine, and I'm not going to let Wes get to me. I up the tempo on the vibe and the crowd responds. Fucking magic.

I sneak another glance. Wes is no longer standing next to Xavier. I'm shocked when a pang of disappointment hits me. Xavier gives me the thumbs up again and smiles like he's won the fucking lottery. I shake away my thoughts and turn back to the crowd. My world.

Liberated, I rip my tank top over my shoulders and wipe the sweat from my face and arms. I circle the shirt above my head before releasing it into the crowd. Hey, it's not just any tank top, one designed by my favorite fashion label. But Xavier has another with him because I do this shit on stage every show.

When I catch a glimpse of the crowd, I can make out the chicks standing in their lace bras. Yeah, we rock this joint. I swipe my forehead, pushing sweat through my hair. My act is almost done so I up the tempo for the last few minutes. Both my hands are busy working the decks, jumping from the mixer to the computer to the turntable, and I finish on the synthesizer, singing on top note. One hand plays the keys, the other points to the crowd. Moving my arm up and down to the beat, I pause for a moment and smile when I hear them join in.

My choir.

When the song ends, I'm covered in sweat and it feels fucking fantastic. I give the peace sign and shout, "Never stop trying, peeps. Stay beautiful, Philly." And then I cross the stage to

Xavier. He throws his arms around me, not caring how disgustingly sweaty I am.

"You rocked it. You fucking rocked it."

I lean my head on his chest and close my eyes, holding onto the emotion rocketing through my body. He's the closest thing I have to family, and I let out a long breath, knowing I have his approval.

"Let's celebrate." He kisses the top of my head. "I have so much I need to talk to you about."

After throwing on a clean shirt, I take his hand and jog down the steps of the stage toward the VIP area. "Let's just head to the hotel to freshen up and then go out."

"I was hoping you'd say that."

"By the way," I ask as we head toward our awaiting vehicle. "What the hell was Wesley doing on my stage?"

"He works here."

"In Philly? Doing what?"

Xavier shrugs. I know that shrug. He's hiding something. "He's working for Marshall Thompson so he's all over the place."

"What the fuck? Since when?" Marshall Thompson owns Red Star, a string of nightclubs around the country. It's *the* club. "Still doesn't tell me what he was doing on *my* stage."

"I wanted to talk to you in private, but I know you won't let up. Wes wants to sign you for weekends at Red Star, and for any festivals they sponsor."

"You're freaking kidding me?" Red Star only hires the hottest name DJs and so far only one of them have been female.

"I kid you not. And Wes also talked about you touring with some big-name artists."

"Since when does Wes work for Marshall Thompson?" If he's disgraced his name and the NFL, how the hell did he score a gig with someone like Marshall?

"It's not something we discussed, Gar. He gave me the details and said to set up a meeting with you tonight."

The moment your dreams fall into place, adrenaline soars through your veins and it's like no other feeling on earth. So why are my insides knotted tight like the rope mooring a boat to a bollard?

"You okay?" Xavier eyes me suspiciously. "That's your third drink in twenty minutes."

"You my fucking dad?"

"If I were, then I wouldn't give a shit what you do."

"Low blow."

"You asked for it." His eyes move to something or someone over my shoulder.

I stiffen, sensing our dinner guests have arrived. After I showered and dressed in something *appropriate*, Xavier and I were picked up in a limo and taken to one of Philly's finest seafood restaurants.

Xavier stands and I follow his lead. A tall man with blondish-gray hair steps into my view. He surveys me quickly before greeting Xavier.

"Mister Brockman, it's good to meet you." Marshall shakes Xavier's hand in a strong, manly way. He then turns to me. "I don't believe I've had the honor of previously meeting you, Miss Delaware."

I give him my best smile before offering my hand. "A pleasure, Mister Thompson." I cringe when his firm handshake crunches my fingers together.

"And you're familiar with Mister Black."

Then *he's* beside me. "Yes. I've had the pleasure of meeting Mister Brockman and Miss Delaware previously." Wes holds out his hand to Xavier and they shake hands. I watch curiously.

Then Wes turns to me, offering his hand. "It's good to see you again, Miss Delaware."

"Please call me Garnet." My tone is sharp. All the courtesies are getting on my last nerve.

Xavier shoots me a look before turning to Marshall Thompson. "Please sit, gentlemen. Wesley has given me a brief description of your offer, but Garnet would like to hear the details tonight before contracts are discussed in depth."

Marshall's eyes swoop toward me. "Well, let me start by saying how surprised I am that Wes found you. How have you slipped under my radar, Garnet?" He smiles like the cat that has a canary in his mouth, and like Wes, his expression makes me a little nervous. I shake it off, knowing the ball is in my court.

"I've been getting plenty of gigs, Mister Thompson, so you might need to check your radar." Xavier coughs at my response. Marshall's smile only broadens.

"You are a surprising package. I thought you had short black hair and dressed in ripped jeans?"

I straighten in my seat and casually down the vodka shot sitting in front of me. "I did. It grew, and I colored it blonde. I like change. A certain look doesn't define who you are."

Out the corner of my eye, I see Wes place a hand to his mouth. But I don't focus on it. I'm busy eyeballing Marshall-fucking-Thompson.

"Yet you brand your skin. That look defines you and marks you for life." He raises one brow at me. My whole body stiffens at his apparent distaste in tattoos. It's the way he says 'brand' that has the hairs on the back of my neck pricking. Hell, I'm not a walking billboard. I don't advertise that I'm gay or a DJ by a certain look, a certain hairstyle, or by my ink. My tattoos signify more. Every one details a moment in my life where I beat the dark shadows, conquered my thoughts, and took a step in a new direction. I want to say 'fuck you,' but before I respond, he adds, "But your style tonight... your dress, well, it's a pleasant surprise."

"This dress was Xavier's choice, not mine. Believe me when I say I'm more comfortable in jeans."

Xavier clears his throat. "What Garnet means is she has a certain style, and many fashion labels send their clothes just so she'll be photographed wearing their brand."

"Your extensive social media following hasn't gone unnoticed, Miss Delaware."

"Garnet," I answer quickly.

"Your popularity may have slipped under my faulty radar"—he eyes me before continuing—"but regardless, I'm sure you'll find my offer too good to refuse."

Wes butts in. "You have heard of Jimmy Sax?"

I roll my eyes. "Do I live on Jupiter?"

Wes grins. "He's also heard of you and wants you to open for him when he tours next year." His grin turns into that heart-stopping smile.

"For real?" I croak. For once, I'm lost for words.

"Very much so," Marshall adds. "And I believe Wes has mentioned the position at Red Star on weekends, and performing at any live concerts we sponsor?"

I nod, still stuck on the possibility of opening for Jimmy Sax.

"Well, I'll leave Wes to discuss matters further and answer any of your questions. Once you've agreed, we can arrange for a contract to be drawn up. As for tonight, I think we can forget the formalities and get to know each other better." Marshall signals to the waiter. "Give me a bottle of your most expensive champagne, young man."

5

garnet

wo hours later, I'm still at the bar with Wes.

Go figure.

Marshall and Xavier have left us to "bond" and discuss some of the lighter details. Xavier is a health freak and often heads to bed early, while Marshall has an early morning flight to San Francisco. Being alone with Wes is not ideal, but he's been nothing but professional up until this point.

"You know what surprises me?" he says after we clink glasses. "You didn't drop the f-bomb once with Marshall."

I roll my eyes. "I know when to act like a lady. Haven't you seen my interviews on YouTube?"

Wes runs a finger along my arm, my skin tingling under his touch. "I have. Every one of them. And I know you can act like a lady. In fact, I intend to see your lady act... in private."

And A-hole Wes is back. "Then I wouldn't be a lady." I knock back another vodka shot.

"Underneath your armor, I know you." He tweaks my nipple and catches my piercing between his fingers.

I squeak and slap his hand. "Fuck off, Wes. I was starting to like you and thought possibly you were a gentleman."

His gaze is fixed on my tits. I didn't wear a bra since the back of the dress is cut low.

Wes' gaze darts back to mine and the intensity burns into me like lasers. "I'm no gentleman."

"Try to keep this meeting professional." I pour more vodka from the bottle in front of me and throw it back like it's water.

"The meeting has closed, Gar." Wes fills my shot glass.

I throw it back. "Then let's talk about you. Why did you fuck up your life for drugs?"

Wes narrows his eyes at me. "Tonight is not about my past. It's about your future."

"If we're gonna work together, I need to know about you...to know I can trust you. Considering you fucked up your life, why should I trust you with mine?"

Wes takes my hand and places it between his. "I know you'll find this hard to believe, but I actually care about you and your future. Yeah, I've been stupid, but I have a chance to help make your dreams come true."

"I'm doing fine without your help."

"You are. Except you're stagnant. If it weren't for my influence on Marshall, he would've given the gig to Tyra Shaun."

I cringe at the mere mention of my rival. "So why the sudden interest in me?"

"Trust me, it's not sudden. I've been following you for a while and I'm well aware of your potential."

"You think I've got what it takes?"

"I know it. What separates you from other DJs is your distinct voice. You can also sing, baby. Like really hit the high notes."

I'm flattered. Over the night, I've warmed to Wes. "Thank you." It's not the first time I've received a compliment about my voice. "Order a round of ABC shots. I've just decided to get fucked up. The best way to celebrate." I wink at him. "I'm just going to the"—I cough—"ladies' room."

I don't need to go, but I want to call Lena and tell her my news out of the earshot of Wes.

"Hi, baby."

"Gar." I can hear the excitement in her voice. "I saw you on MTV. Your gig looked awesome."

"It was fucking awesome. I'm still out celebrating. Marshall-fucking-Thompson has offered me a contract to work weekends at Red Star and to open for Jimmy Sax when he tours next year."

Lena gasps loudly into the phone. "What?"

"Yeah, apparently Wes Black works for him, and he's been following me on social media. He's been to a few of my gigs and was at the festival today. He's been talking to Marshall and tonight I agreed to work for him."

"Wow. That happened fast. Hey, I've seen Wes at some of your shows, but I didn't think anything of it."

"Well, I just wanted to share it with you." My voice breaks at the end—damn I miss her.

"Thank you," she whispers. "I'm so proud of you."

"Yeah? How proud?"

"I want to reach into the phone and touch you, make-you-feel-good proud?"

I head into the stall, lean on the wall and pull my dress up around my hips. "Touch me

where?" I whisper. I hear movement over the phone. "Are you at your Mom's?"

"Yes. I'm just heading to my bedroom." I want to argue that her bedroom is at my house, but now is not the time. A moment later, she's breathing heavy and I imagine her touching herself. "I want to lick your clit the way you like. Little circles and then suck hard." I close my eyes and my finger works my clit, rubbing and tweaking.

"And then I'll slip my fingers inside of you and find your special spot, and work that baby until you're writhing under me." I open my legs wider and push my fingers inside of me. They're not as long as Lena's and from this angle hardly do the job, but it's better than nothing. "My tongue and fingers will work you, baby, until you come, over and over in my mouth." Her sweet, dirty voice sends a thrill down my spine and I'm sliding up and down the wall, groaning. "That's it, baby," she whispers.

I hear voices on the other side of the door and my building orgasm fizzles. "I gotta go," I say quickly. "Talk soon, Lena." I end the call, then straighten my dress and open the door before walking past several gaping ladies. I find

Wes at the bar and immediately down both shots.

He arches a brow at me. His expression reminds me of Marshall-fucking-Thompson. "One was for me."

"Order more," I say bluntly.

"You're not having another. You're already fucked up." His voice is rough and demanding.

"That's the idea." I wink at him, but he takes my wink the wrong way.

He leans in—too close—opens his mouth and stops. His forehead furrows and his expression darkens. "I can smell you," he growls.

I frown at him then lift my arm and take a whiff of my pit. "What do you mean? I showered." The room dips and I close my eyes momentarily to regain my balance. "Whoa. Guess the shots have caught up."

Wes grabs my hand and steadies me. He holds it, his thumb skimming across my fingers as he studies them. Then he lifts my hand to his lips and kisses each finger lightly, a deviant smile crossing his face. He moves my fingers under his nose. "Just what were you up to in there, Gar?"

I attempt to pull my hand from his, but he's too strong and keeps it by his lips. Then he slowly slips my fingers inside his mouth, his tongue curling and sucking. I groan loudly, struck with a longing sensation between my thighs. I need my vibrator.

He slips my fingers out of his mouth, the action making my knees weak. Then he bends so his lips are near my ear. "I want you so fucking bad." My hand is still trapped in his and then he slowly places it on his erection pressing against his pants.

Fuck.

"Like I said, I'm not into dicks." I yank my hand from his and this time he lets me go.

"Oh, but I think you could be if you weren't afraid."

My head is spinning and my knees are weak. What the hell is happening? I can usually hold my liquor. But Wes...

"I'm not afraid of you," I say with finality. With my free hand, I support my head.

He towers over me, even when he curls his body over me like a cage. Maybe he's protecting me...or claiming me. "Prove it," he whispers and licks my neck.

Sparks shoot into my abdomen. "This is so fucking wrong," I mutter.

"Yet it's so right. Besides, when have you ever played by the rules?" He sits on a stool positioned behind him and he opens his thighs so I'm almost between them.

I shake my head. "I'm with someone."

"Don't tell me you haven't been with anyone else since you've been with Lena, because I know you're lying." His eyes blaze into mine.

I had. She forgave me. I couldn't hurt her again. "How do you know so much about me?"

"Twitter. Instagram. Facebook. People like to talk about you."

Fuck, has he read the posts from two years ago? My thoughts scramble, but I aim to divert the attention away from me. "Yeah, and they like to talk about you too," I say in a sarcastic tone. When his eyes narrow, I lift my chin, knowing I've found his Achilles. "You're not perfect."

"I'm not trying to be. You and me, we're tarred with the same brush." He rests his hands on my hips to steady me when I stumble in the goddamn heels.

"Don't compare me to you. You might have ruined your career, but you're not getting a chance to mess up mine."

"I'm not trying to fuck up your life, Gar. I'm trying to help you. How the hell do you think you got this meeting tonight?"

"With talent." I shoot him a challenging look.

"Yeah, you've got talent, but unless you have friends like me, it won't get you noticed past a few festivals and second-rate clubs."

"You think I owe you?"

"No." He stares at me long enough that I notice the blue flecks in his green eyes. "I want you to trust me."

"You want to get in my pants and ruin my relationship with my girl. Fuck you."

"I'm not trying to destroy anything." His expression deepens and hell, my body reacts to him. "Off the record...you—I've imagined doing certain things to you, and now I can't stop thinking about it."

Damn the alcohol because I don't have a filter, or as it seems, any common sense when I say, "What things?" I'm always open to kinky.

His hands slide around my hips to my butt and he cups my rear, pulling me close. I stumble and my hands fall on his shoulders to balance myself. "You want me to show you?"

"Nope. I want you to describe it." My heart is racing as adrenaline soars through my veins. Internally, I'm fighting a battle. My body wants more, but somewhere in the back of my confused, intoxicated brain, I have an urge to flee.

I'm not afraid of him.

In a swift action, he yanks me forward and my hips are shoved against his crotch. He dips his head. I let out a sigh when he bypasses my lips and nudges my neck with his nose. His breath tingles my skin as he lifts his mouth to my ear. "This is for your ears only as I'm not a fan of publicity, especially when it comes to whom I fuck."

I attempt to protest that fucking me isn't going to happen when he asks, "What's your favorite sexual position?" My mouth opens and before I comment, I slowly comprehend he's baiting me. "Oh, I'm sorry. I forgot that's a limitation for you."

"Fuck off." I shove his shoulders, but he hardly budges. His face is a mere inch from mine. "I have my ways, and secrets to sexual satisfaction you'll never understand."

"I'm all ears," he sneers.

"Lena gets me, understands my needs, and I hers. You have a one-track mind. Get your cock in my pussy, and once you blow it would be all-over-red-rover. We can orgasm more times than

I can count and never tire. And the accessories easily replace anything you have to offer."

He grabs my hand and places it on his, then curls my slim fingers over his, one finger at a time. I watch him moving my hand, not sure where he's going with it. When I've caressed his third finger, he stills. "Now imagine three of my fingers inside you, hell, imagine four or five, and tell me how much better it would feel than your chick's delicate fingers. As for tiring, I'm an athlete and I don't tire easily. These babies"—he wiggles his fingers in front of my face—"are a strong, working man's hand."

I slap his hand away. "You know what I think when guys talk themselves up? Their dicks are the size of my pinky."

Wes snickers. "You just had your hand on my cock. You and I both know that's not the case."

Yeah, he's right and I'm sick of him making me squirm. "I've heard enough. I think I'll call it a night."

"You proved me right. You're scared."

I jerk away. "Of you? Don't fucking kid yourself. I'm going to say it again. I'm not into *you*."

"And I'm going to say it again. I don't care. I like a challenge and I'll finger you all night if you want me to."

"What the hell is wrong with you?" I turn on my heel and head for the door.

He easily catches up to me. His arm goes around my waist, guiding me. I don't push him away, instead I lean on him for balance when we walk past security. "That wasn't an invitation," I mutter.

"I know. But I told Xavier I'd get you home safely and we're staying at the same hotel."

"Convenient."

"Courtesy of Marshall Thompson," he says dryly.

So he shares the same opinion of Marshall as me.

Inside the cab, I keep my distance. After a few minutes, I ask, "Why are you being nice to me? I mean, clearly you're not getting any."

He turns and stares out the window. "I told you. I'm trying to help you."

I nod wearily, consciousness slowly slipping away. "And there's nothing in it for you?"

"Oh, there's definitely something in it for me. I get the respect of Marshall when you sign and that holds a lot of weight. I also get to spend more time with you." He reaches out and touches my hand resting on the leather seat between us. I don't shift it until we're back at the hotel.

My head feels like it's made of lead, and my bones as if they've evaporated. Fuck, I feel like a lightweight, the extra shots wreaking havoc with my brain.

Wes helps me from the car and drapes an arm over my shoulder as we walk into the vast foyer. My gaze remains focused on the marble floor as we pass more security. Finally, we reach the elevator.

Inside the elevator, I flop against his chest. I could fall asleep standing up. The doors open and I peer through one eye to see the long hallway to my room. Fumbling, I retrieve my keycard from my clutch and hand it to him.

"Okay," Wes says as he pushes open the door with one hand, keeping the other firmly around my waist. He guides me into the room and I collapse onto the bed. "Hold up, Gar." Wes rolls me over and starts to unzip me.

"What the fuck," I moan.

"Do you want to sleep in your dress?"

"No. Get it off me." I keep my eyes closed as Wes slides the straps over my shoulders, then I lift my rear and feel the material as it slides down my legs. All inhibition lost, thanks to the shots.

I hear him hiss and I roll onto my side. His hand trails down my arm, touching the artwork costing me mega bucks. His fingers trail to my hips, across my stomach to my navel. I sense him tracing the stem of the rose, his touch traveling lower.

"May I?" he whispers.

I'm too exhausted to give it much thought. "Yes."

garnet

y eyes flutter open, and not because I want to wake up. My damn head is throbbing like a bitch and my mouth is parched. My tongue is swollen and tastes foul.

A weight lies heavily across my side, and a large hand is draped across my breast. My gaze darts lower to my naked body where the tattooed hand rolls my nipple ring between thick fingers. I recognize the letters FLY inked onto the three largest fingers.

I blink, comprehending... remembering.

A soft kiss lands on my shoulder. "You awake?"

Fuck!

Panic floods my mind. Throwing the sheet back, I spring from the bed and stare down at

Wes lying naked, the sheet sitting at his hips. In a second, his beauty crosses my mind but I can't think straight. Not with this damn stabbing pain in my head and the thought of what I supposedly did, and *why* I can't remember. "What the fuck are you doing here?"

Wes' eyes round. My gaze darts around the room and lands on a box of condoms placed near the bedside lamp next to him.

"What. The. Fuck."

Wes follows my line of sight to the condoms and a smirk plays across his lips. "Two left. You told me to save them for morning." He lifts the sheet invitingly and I catch a glimpse of his hard-on. Without thinking, my hand travels between my legs and I gently touch myself.

"Oh, you'll be sore, baby. Turns out, you weren't afraid after all."

My chest tightens in realization and my heart speeds up. Emotions hit me like a tidal wave and my stomach plummets as I think about Lena.

Wes' devil gaze travels down my body and I know he's staring at the rose. I have a brief recollection of him touching me...

"I did whatever you told me to do. It was all your idea."

"My idea?" I shout accusingly, the disbelief clear in my tone.

Wes nods once. "Yeah. What the hell's wrong?"

My hands clutch at my hair. I can't breathe as a vision of last night hits me... wrapped in Wes' arms, I'm sated and happy as he fucks me slowly, lovingly.

No, no, no, no.

"You have to leave." Wes opens his mouth to speak, but I cut him off. "Now."

He jumps out of bed and walks toward me. I'm ogling his body, the hard lines of muscles and the ink. It's too much and I back away. "No," I say firmly.

"Gar, it's not what it looks like." He gives me a wounded expression, but I shake my head.

"You mean we didn't fuck?" I ask, raising my eyebrows. His lips press into a hard line. He doesn't need to answer because I'm now aware of a steady pulse in my pussy. "I'm taking a shower. I need you to be gone by the time I get out." I stop myself from sprinting to the bathroom, then I somehow manage to close the door without slamming it. I sink to the cold tiles and land on my knees, blocking out the images of me on top of Wes, grinding my hips and talking to him as though we were a couple.

All I can think about is Lena.

What the fuck have I done?

7

garnet

wo weeks on and I'm struggling. The headaches, the sharp pains in my chest, the constant feeling as though my stomach is home to a thousand snakes tangling their bodies as they wrestle inside of me. But most of all, I'm struggling with the guilt.

I fell apart after my DJ gig in New York, and Xavier—my manager and best friend—demanded answers. So now Xavier is the only person who knows what happened, apart from the obvious.

Wesley Black.

My head hurts to even think his name.

Then my breath quickens as questions whirl at the back of my mind, followed by an internal battle of what to do to make things right. Anything to erase the dark thoughts eating away at my sanity.

No, I haven't told Lena.

No, I'm not speaking to Wes.

Yes, I still have to work with him. Although I signed a deal with Marshall Thompson, CEO of Wes' company, I figured his job was done and I would no longer have to deal with him.

Yes, I was wrong.

Mother fucking wrong.

"You should ease up on that," Xavier says after I swig antacid straight from the plastic container. "At least use a measuring cup."

"I can't function when my fucking guts are on fire." I take another swig.

"You have to fix this. After tonight's concert, you're getting on a plane and going home."

"And do what? Confess? What the hell do I tell her when I barely remember?" I screw the lid on the bottle and throw it at my open handbag in the corner of the room.

"Talk to her, goddammit. Regardless of what happens, you can't continue to work like this. You'll end up in the ER."

I roll my eyes. "The past two weeks is the soberest I've been in years." No drugs. No alcohol. If I want to impress Marshall fucking Thompson, then I need to stay focused… and sober. The latter to ensure I don't accidentally fall into bed with Wes—again. And although I can't remember a hell of a lot about that night, my stomach churns at the thought that it could have been the best fucking sex of my life.

My loss, or gain, depending on which way you look at it.

Xavier rubs the back of his neck. "Being sober is a good thing."

Bull fucking shit to that. My whole body hurts and I tremble as though I'm sitting on an active San Andreas Fault. But I keep my mouth shut. Xavier's like a big brother—the closest thing I have to family—and I hate the thought of disappointing him.

"Those dark rings under your eyes are a giveaway you're not sleeping. You need a break. Even if you don't talk about what happened, at least go home and see Lena. We have a weeklong break after the show today."

I nod and ignore the urge to chug more antacid. "You're right. I don't need to tell her, since I don't even know what happened."

Xavier cocks an eyebrow at me. "Gar—"

"Just book me the damn flight."

I don't recall much about the night in Philly after I fell onto the bed of my hotel room, thanks to my stupid decision to celebrate by downing an excessive amount of shots. Wes said he had only acted on what I'd told him to do, and unfortunately nothing from my limited recollections disproves his claim. I recently remembered grabbing Wes by his tie and pulling him onto the bed, asking him to kiss me. I instigated everything. Since then, snippets of the night have come back to me, but I've pushed the memories aside, not wanting to relive it out of guilt.

Lena has told me more than once that my libido goes through the roof after a night out getting wrecked. Wes didn't need to confirm it. The almost empty packet of condoms beside him and my throbbing pussy left no doubt in my mind.

Fuck!

Rubbing my hands up and down my jean-clad thighs, I think of what to say to Lena. My stomach rumbles and I'm sure I'll barf before the day is out. Glancing down at my hands, I stare at my trembling fingers. Sometimes I wish I were more like my mother, who was exceptionally good at not caring about the feelings of other people.

The last thing I want to do is hurt Lena. She's my world, and I can't imagine life without her.

Yet here I am, waiting to go onstage at a music festival in Charlotte with a smorgasbord of emotion coursing through me, thinking about how one dumb action has the potential to change my life—and not for the better. The band finishes and I make my way up the stairs to the back of the stage. I find a chair behind a curtain and wait while the area is cleared and made ready for me.

A crowd is building. Seeing the fans usually gets me pumped, but I'm feeling so much other fucking shit, I'm sure my pleasure pathways are blocked. Beside the chair, I see a pen sitting on a notepad. One of the stage crew's checklist. I pick up the pen and trace the outline of a rose inked onto my forearm. Without realizing, I press harder, pushing the pen into my skin until it burns. I close my eyes and move the pen back and forth, the sharp pain a distraction to everything else I'm feeling.

It feels good. I concentrate solely on the sting biting into my arm.

"What the fuck are you doing?"

The sound of Wes' voice pulls me away from the pleasurable pain. I spring from my chair, putting distance between us. "I thought I told you to stay the fuck away from me."

Wes pushes his hands into his pant pockets. "Kind of hard when we work together. You've ignored me for two whole weeks. There are things we need to talk about."

"If it's business, then talk to Xavier," I bite back.

His gaze lowers and I'm aware of blood trickling down my arm. I rub away the evidence, the red blending in with my inked sleeve. Wes grabs my arm. I try to pull it away, but—what can I say?—the guy's a football player. He studies my forearm. "What the fuck?"

"Don't say a damn thing." This time when I yank my arm away, he releases me.

"I have an obligation to look out for you. If something's wrong, I need to know. Otherwise Marshall will have my balls."

"Ironic, don't you think, when you're the cause of my problems. And thanks for the tip."

"For Christ sakes, Gar, it was just sex."

"Yeah, must have been pretty forgettable since I don't remember much. Plus, I'm glad it didn't mean shit to you. Takes the pressure off when I tell Lena it meant nothing." I stare at him a moment before turning back to the stage.

"It did and you know it," he says, low and deep. "And you can't blame me that you don't remember." He takes a step closer and his gaze burns into me.

His words hit me like a wrecking ball of guilt. "Get off my fucking stage!" I scream at him, but he doesn't move.

Wes stares me down. "You. Will. Talk. To. Me," he says, articulating each word slowly. "Tonight." Then he walks his tight, perfectly shaped ass off the stage.

8

wes

hat. The. Fuck.

If I'm causing her that much pain, I need to fix it.

I storm off to a corner and stand out of her line of sight but close enough to watch Garnet perform. The fans love her charisma. I know Marshall is impressed with me signing Gar, but it's not him I want to please. The fiery blonde on stage has my cock constantly jumping to attention, and now that I've had a taste of her, it's like shooting up with that first syringe of heroin...there's no going back. She's my fucking kryptonite.

My head is ready to explode with frustration that she won't talk to me. Christ, she hates breathing the same air as me. But it will change. It has to...

I close my eyes. After attending all her shows, I know her tracks like the back of my hand, and right now is the part when Garnet adds her own touch and sings. It's like listening to an angel. She has no idea how fucking unbelievably talented she is. And I'm going to help her tap that talent and reach her potential to be the star she deserves. Like a man possessed, I'm on a mission to help her succeed.

Again.

Hell, she has me and she doesn't even know it. I tell myself it's a way of redeeming myself; to make up for the stupid-ass way I fucked up my own career. That now I have a chance to do something right. But it's more and I know it.

I've had a deep-seeded infatuation with Garnet since I kissed her nine years ago. Even when she was just a lost sixteen-year-old, hanging out in dodgy nightclubs in West Hollywood with a fake ID, she knew she wanted to be a DJ. When I heard her sing her heart out—high on some shit—and saw the dream in her blue eyes, the raw emotion casting a sky-blue haze over me, I wanted to bottle it up.

Over the years, my life spiraled out of control but I continued to watch her from the sidelines. Garnet partied hard like every other performer;

she simply didn't let it interfere with her work. Even when I was at my lowest—knew I was going to be drug tested and knew damn sure I was going to be found guilty—I watched her perform at the Rox only hours before my test. Mesmerized, I stood in a corner, ignoring every asshole that came up to me trying to spark a conversation about football. I was fucked, so was my career, and all I wanted was to watch Garnet on stage. I waited for her to sing to me as if I were the only one in the room. I fed off her energy, her passion, and her ability to hold onto her dream. She was a shining light in a dark club. And since then, I've needed her light to guide me out of a dark tunnel.

My phone vibrates in my pocket. I open the text from Marshall, aka Daddy Number One.

Be in my office by four.

That's it. No '*how are you*?' after his quick trip back to San Fran.

My biological father has set the rules of my new life and I'm a pawn in his fucked-up game. Growing up I didn't have hardly anything to do with him—or vice-versa—after he left my mother when I was two and she remarried a year later. Her new husband became Daddy Number Two. Marshall simply paid the bills. But when he heard I was accepting a college football scholarship, Marshall magically appeared back in my life. After my mega fuck-up reflected on him and caused major embarrassment, he set new ground rules. Work for him and do what he says or end up behind bars.

Yet it's not Marshall Thompson saving me.

It's Garnet.

And I need her more than the air I breathe.

Reeling in my thoughts, I shoot a look at Xavier, who's standing on the side of the stage. Xavier's protective stance reminds me of my college team's left tackle. With legs slightly apart and his arms folded across his broad chest, he'll do anything to protect Gar, but he also knows I want the best for her career. It's my other intentions I need to convince him of, and at the moment he's staring at me like he wants to cut off my fucking cock.

Swallowing, I walk up and stand beside him. "This is only the beginning, man. Her career is really going to take off."

Xavier juts out his chin at me. "So the best thing you can do now is leave her the fuck alone."

Before I answer, he adds, "She's leaving tomorrow to go home to LA for a few days. To

Lena," he adds. "She has to get her head back in the game before the show in Atlanta. And she has to do it without you fucking messing with her head. So I'm warning you, stay the hell away."

My chest tightens on hearing she wants to escape me. I stare down coolly at Xavier. No bastard will tell me what to do when it comes to Garnet. Then my gaze finds her, one hand raised in the air pumping to the beat of her music. Her other hand is working the deck. Her sweet little hips are swaying and grinding a little. I remember how she grinded her sweet pussy on my cock.

She turns and her blue eyes latch onto mine. For a moment, I feel the joy—the high—she is experiencing.

She's my fucking drug.

"Sorry, mate. No. Can. Do."

9

garnet

Walking into my empty apartment fills me with relief and not the loneliness I anticipated. I'm fatigued, and not only in the physical sense. The pilot met his fair share of turbulence flying across the damn continent so I sat with my stomach contents rising and my heart in my throat for the entire flight.

I need to calm myself before Lena arrives. Everything is the way it was and I assume Lena hasn't paid a visit since I left. My teeth clench thinking about Lena's mother. She's such a judgmental bitch. In the three years I've been with Lena, her Mom still looks at me as though I've brainwashed Lena into joining a cult.

After dumping my dirty clothes in the laundry room, I walk back into the kitchen just as the front door opens. Lena bounds in, wearing a broad smile that removes any doubt from my mind that coming home was a mistake.

Lena jumps into my arms and kisses me. "I've missed you," she says, out of breath.

"Me too." My hand slips under her top and finds her breast, soft and full.

In mere seconds we're naked, hands all over each other, lips mashed together. I catch a whiff of her, slightly musky and sweaty, and I think about the nervous sweat covering my body as I've contemplated what to tell her.

"Baby, I need to shower," I whisper.

"I'll join you," she says. "I hate Mom's bathroom so I didn't bother showering this morning."

I lean back. "You didn't have to stay there. You can come home anytime, even just to shower."

"Let's not talk about this now." She takes my hand and leads me to the bathroom. "You're home. That's the main thing."

"And you're not brainwashed." I grin, but it's not really funny.

"Don't, Gar." Lena turns on the taps. "I love my Mom. I wish you had a better relationship with yours so you could understand."

I snort. That's not happening. "Did she try to convince you to go home to live?"

Lena reaches up and her hand brushes over my face, then she pulls me under the shower with her. Her avoiding the question is the answer I'm seeking. My gut tightens as frustration boils up inside of me. "Relax," Lena whispers, soaping up my breasts. Her hands move to my shoulders. "So tense, baby." I close my eyes and focus on her fingers easing the tension out of my muscles. "Tell me about the tour."

I open my eyes and see her gentle smile. Her eager expression relaxes me a fraction. "What part?"

"Start with your meeting with Marshall Thompson. How cool is that? And now we get to hang out at Red-friggin-Star, the best club in Hollywood. You're the real star here, Gar."

I grin at her. "You think I'm cool?"

"Oh, baby. You're more than cool. You're the best. I'm so proud of you."

Her words fall on my ears like a prayer sent from heaven. "Proud of me," I repeat in a low, croaky voice. It's all I ever wanted. I drop to my knees and kiss her mound. "Open for me, baby."

Lena spreads her legs and leans back against the wall, giving me a better angle to access her pussy. I suck on her clit and she moans, clamping her hands in my hair. I flick my tongue before tasting her, the sound of her moans urging me on. The shower beats down on my back, a sting I welcome. Listening to her voice whispering my name and the way her hands tangle in my wet hair, the heat and the steam surrounding us, I'm lost in the moment... in us. It all seems real at last, and I momentarily forget about Wesley Black.

When Lena comes, I push up from my knees. Her head falls back on the white tiles, air rushing from her lungs. I kiss her breast, taking her nipple slowly into my mouth, teasing her.

"What's it like working with them?" she asks, breathless.

"Who?" I'm not interested in talking about work, and I'm a little thrown she is thinking about it now, just moments after I gave her an amazing orgasm.

"Wesley Black and Marshall Thompson, of course."

I straighten, step back, and stare at her. "Why?"

Lena shrugs. It's a small movement, and if she wasn't naked I might have missed it. "They're, you know, important. Famous."

I make a non-committal noise. "They're just people. The famous part makes them bigger ass-holes. I only talk to them when I *have* to." I swallow hard as the memory of Wes lying naked in my bed jumps into my head.

Her eyes meet mine. "It must have been ex-citing having dinner with them, talking about your future. Wes wanting you."

I jerk away when she utters those last words.

My expression startles her, and she places a hand on my shoulder. "Do you realize how im-portant you are to them if they wine and dine you and offer a contract? You're very lucky, Gar. You've been given a great opportunity. Don't blow it. I know what you're like with guys like Black and Thompson. You despise them and push them away at every opportunity. Your smart mouth can be your downfall."

My gaze shoots to the white tiles on the shower floor. I focus on the water pooling around the drain.

"Hey, all I'm saying is give these guys a break. Don't ruin your future because you hate on al-pha males."

I give her a sideways glance. Lena rubs my arm. "Come on, let's go out and celebrate." She kisses my cheek and pushes open the glass door, steps out, and wraps a towel around her, leaving me alone.

I remain under the shower a moment longer, the hot beads of water massaging my aching back. I try to will away the dark thoughts crossing my mind, but I can't help feeling cheated with Lena getting out of the shower after being away from her for so long.

Sitting on the black lounge in the club, I laugh on cue with my friends. It's been months since I've hung out at Velvet, a prominent club in downtown LA. The whole gang is here, minus Xavier. Lena thought that hooking us all up at our old stomping crowd to celebrate my success would be an ideal reunion, especially since I haven't seen some of my gal pals for a year. It's been all work and no time for friends. Only Lena. And I guess she's been lonely. But I'm not gonna lie, I'm not feeling it tonight. I'm tired and was hoping for some quiet down time with my girl.

Sheila makes a joke about some straight guy's fashion sense and the gang laughs. I haven't seen Lena laugh this much in months. Maybe I have been neglecting her for my work, but my work comes first.

Lena pulls me into her side and rubs my thigh. "You having a good time?"

I give her my biggest smile. "Sure am, baby."

She lifts a hand and rubs my face. "You sure? I thought you'd be happy to see everyone..."

"I am, I am," I say quickly. "Thank you for arranging this for me."

Lena assesses my eyes then she leans in, her lips caressing mine. I open my mouth and her tongue dives in. Lena's kiss is slow, sensual, and hot. My fingers massage her thigh, creeping higher. Her hand finds my tit and she caresses it gently through the loose cotton material, toying with the ring.

"Girl is sex-deprived being on the road," Peta calls out. I let go of Lena and flick her the bird. Lena pulls away and straddles me, her thighs open and her short dress stretches tight. I have easy access to her pussy. She places her hands on my shoulders and stares down at me, a wicked expression crossing her face. My gaze flicks around the group. Our friends are no longer paying us any attention. Peta's chatting with Kate. Sheila and Becky have already locked faces. David and Kurt look to be in a serious discussion.

My gaze travels back to Lena's heated expression. Slowly my hand travels up her leg along her inner thigh to a scrappy piece of material. And it's soaked. Lena lowers her head, pushes my baseball cap back away from my eyes, and mashes her lips with mine.

Two of my fingers skim her entrance. Her pussy is warm, wet, and soft as satin cushions. Tucking my elbow to my hip, I rotate my arm, my fingers curling up and in, finding the spot that makes her gasp against my lips.

"Harder," she whispers, her tone sounding like a dare.

I grin at her, rubbing her core. She lifts her rear a fraction then pushes down on my hand, her forehead pressing against mine. She's no longer kissing me. Her lips are close to mine, simply inhaling the air I breathe out. She's panting fast and soon she sighs deliciously and stops, her body relaxing as her limbs become limp.

Smiling, I remove my fingers from her crotch, tighten my arms around her back, and nestle my head into her shoulder. "Love you, baby."

⁂

My bag is packed. I'm watching Lena pack up some of her things before she heads to work. She's returning to her mother's home for the remainder of my tour, claiming it's because it's closer to the boutique where she works.

My chest is tight. My stomach churns. I don't want to say anything and start a fight. And I don't want to leave Lena. I'm afraid her mom will sink her claws into her and I'll lose her.

And if I'm being honest with myself, the thought of facing Wes again scares me. I'm afraid of where my scrambled emotions are leading me. A few days ago, Lena sensed my uneasiness and talked up the importance of maintaining a business relationship with Wes and Marshall.

I repeat her words over and over in my head. It's business, nothing more.

"You okay?" she asks, touching my hands.

Sitting on the bed and staring at nothing, I glance up into her big blue eyes. "Yeah. Just thinking."

"Do you have your period?"

I blink. "What?"

"You seem off, and you're due. I started bleeding like a bitch this morning and you normally get yours a few days before me. But after last night, I knew you hadn't started yet."

My mouth opens, then I close it again. I shrug dismissively. "I'm a few days late. Guess with all the late nights and stress of the shows, I'm thrown out of rhythm."

Lena pats my hand. "When we go shopping today, you should buy some multi-vitamins."

I nod and force myself to smile.

"Gar?" Lena stares at me. She touches my forehead with the back of her hand. "You're burning up."

"I feel like shit," I say honestly.

"Come on. Let's get you some aspirin." She takes my hand and leads me into the kitchen. I'm going to need a lot more than fucking aspirin to calm myself.

Lena's assistant covered for her at lunch so she could accompany me to LAX airport. Sitting beside her at my gate, I'm staring at the nearby shops, particularly the pharmacy... thinking.

"I'm just heading to the restrooms," Lena whispers. "Meet you back here."

Next thing I know, I'm standing in an aisle with a packet of Ibuprofen in my hand, staring at the pregnancy kits. Can I actually do it? Buying the kit seems like admitting to myself that I actually fucked up, and at the moment denial is my best coping mechanism.

"Gar?" I turn to Lena to find an odd look on her face. Her gaze flickers to the shelf I'm ogling and then to me.

"Got it," I say quickly, holding up the packet of Ibuprofen. Then I turn on my heel and march to the counter, my heart thumping against my rib cage.

Lena says nothing as we wait by my departure gate. When boarding for my Atlanta flight is announced, she stands beside me, taking my hand. "Call me when you arrive." I nod. "I'll miss you."

"I'll miss you too." I swallow a lump in my throat. "I don't want to leave." It's the truth. In addition to not wanting to leave Lena, I hate flying. I don't say anything because I'm not a pussy.

Lena throws her arms around me and kisses me on the lips. I drop my bag to the floor. My arms circle her tiny waist and I kiss her back.

To hell with onlookers.

When I release her, she sneaks another kiss on my cheek. "Call me," she says softly, but it's an instruction.

I walk past some elderly ladies who are staring at me as though I have two heads.

Whatever.

I head straight to the front of the line. Business class, baby. I feel like giving them the bird.

But I don't because I know how frigid some of the old ducks are. Attracting more attention to myself is the last thing I need. Lena's positive words echo in my head.

So I shoot them my best smile and say in my sweetest voice, "Good afternoon, ladies."

When their gazes lower to the ink on my arms, I know I haven't fooled them.

wes

I stalk away from the stage after watching Garnet perform. The end is my favorite when she loses her top and throws it to the crowd.

Yeah, I'm a sick bastard.

My joy is superficial, knowing she still fucking hates me and I'm lost as to how to make things right. The skin on my back crawls like fucking ants are all over me.

I know what I need and where to get it.

After finding Stefan and paying more for the hit because I'm not a 'client'—motherfucker— I saunter off toward a bathroom in the VIP area. Before I make it, a chick from one of the less popular bands calls out to me. I stop and stare at her, trying to recall her name. *Fail.* But I really don't give a fuck because all I want is this cocaine and some privacy so I can feel some joy over the pain of seeing Gar's hateful glare boring into my gut.

Band girl springs up beside me, and I don't miss the way her tits bounce in her low-cut top. She puts an arm around my waist, then looks up at me with bright eyes. "I just saw you with Stefan."

"So?" I turn away and keep walking, but her hand remains around my waist.

"I also have a hit."

I shrug. "Whatever."

We find a bathroom and close the door. After clearing a spot near the sink, I sprinkle the powder in a heap. I pull out my business card and use the edge to make two neat lines. Band girl empties her packet. I hand her my card and she repeats my action before passing back the card. After replacing it in my wallet, I retrieve a hundred dollar bill, roll it tightly, then lean down and snort the first line. I hand her the rolled note and she snorts her line before handing me back the note and I snort the second line.

Leaning against the wall, I close my eyes and surrender to the bright colors. My limbs lighten and I feel I could actually fucking fly. My heart swells, the pain momentarily forgotten. My energy level hits the ceiling, and I'm ready to walk back out and face anything Gar throws at me. My hand swipes away powder from my nose, and I turn and open the door a fraction. Through the gap, I notice the lounge area is empty.

"Wait." Band girl grabs my hand, pulls me back, and I release the doorknob. She walks a few steps back until her rear hits the basin. She places my hand over her perky tit. No bra. Her tits are fake. I've touched enough to know the difference. She loops both arms around my neck. "We're not done yet."

I'm about to tell her to stop, but she drops to her knees and unzips my fly quicker than the words can leave my tongue. *Fuck you, cocaine.*

Band girl's mouth is around my cock and I'm groaning, rocking my hips with my hands in her sweaty hair. Her tongue is like magic, casting a spell over the room so that only her mouth and my cock exist. As she works me, I realize that a release is exactly what I need to take my mind off Garnet, Marshall—everything.

I clamp my eyes shut and try to enjoy the moment, imagining it's Gar's mouth around my dick. I'm going to need more than band girl's mouth to come because this is one hell of a boner.

My eyes open slightly, and I peer at my reflection in the mirror above the sink. Apart from the pathetic look on my face, I look normal, dressed in a white shirt buttoned up to the collar in a respectable way. The suit jacket hangs on a hook beside me. The sink obscures me from the waist down so I can only feel the cock sucking, not see it.

My eyes flicker to the door reflected in the mirror. It's slightly ajar. Then I see *her,* standing there watching us through the gap.

I'm too high to care. She hates me—wants to erase any memory of us together. This will help. And for some idiotic reason, knowing Gar is watching, seeing what she is missing out on, spurs me on. Now that I've caught her, I assume she won't hang around to watch.

Linking my fingers around band girl's jaw, I say, "Enough." I pull her up and spin her around so her hands are on the basin. Yanking her tight, short skirt around her waist, I find she's not wearing any panties.

"You want this?" I ask as I pull a condom from my pocket, always ready for an opportunity to fuck. I rip open the packet with my teeth while watching band girl's face in the mirror.

"Yes," she whispers. Her eyes shut and she moans, wiggling her ass in anticipation.

I don't even check if she's wet.

Just as I slam into her, I check the door.

Fuck.

Gar is still there, watching me, her sweet lips slightly parted. I'm relentless, ramming myself into band girl, the slapping noise echoing off the walls of the restroom. This time Garnet's eyes meet mine in the mirror. She stares back at me, her blue eyes slightly rounded. We stare long enough to know it's no mistake that I've busted her.

I only break my gaze when band girl's hand reaches behind and touches my thigh. I slap her hand away and place it back on the sink.

We are fucking. Nothing else.

This girl doesn't get to touch me like Garnet did, even though Gar doesn't remember a fucking thing. The anger of Gar not remembering one of the best nights of my life goads me on, seeking the pleasure I desperately need.

My gaze shoots back to the door. She's still there. This time I shake my head at her. I don't want her to see me come. Not like this. I'm fucking, nothing more.

I hear voices and the door quickly closes. Hell, Gar is guarding the door for me. I have to make this quick. I reach around and press on band girl's clit. She squeals a little and her cunt tightens around my cock. Perfect. I do it again and again until I release my load inside of her.

It only takes a few minutes for me to catch my breath—one of the perks of having years of football training. I pull out unceremoniously, then walk to a bathroom stall and drop the condom in the toilet and flush it. When I walk back, band girl is adjusting her clothing and trying her best to look sexy.

"If you need a minute, I'll stand guard on the other side," I tell her.

"Wes." She lifts an arm and reaches for my face.

My fingers latch onto her wrist and stop her from touching me. "We fucked. It was nice. We're high. Don't expect anything more," I warn. "I'll give you a minute." People gather in the lounge. My hand goes to my pocket and I fiddle with my wallet. When I'm sure no one is heading this way, I walk by and outside for some fresh air.

My eyes burn when the sun hits me with force. I rip my sunglasses from my jacket pocket and place them over my sensitive eyes. My heart is racing, but it's not only from the high. Realization has settled in as to what I just did—and more importantly, *who* was watching—and I'm no longer feeling as invincible as I did ten minutes ago.

If she loathed me before, she'll hate me even more now.

My ears prick to the beautiful sound of a female voice and the steady beat of drums. I head in the direction of the music, lean against a barricade, and watch one of the supporting acts. The lead singer is brilliant and obviously has raw talent, but she's not as talented as Gar. If Gar didn't want her DJ gig so bad, she could easily front a band.

"She's good, isn't she?"

My eyes round behind my sunglasses at Garnet standing beside me. She's the last person I expected to see.

garnet

hand Wes a bottle of water. "Thought you could use this." I know first-hand the importance of staying hydrated after a hit. And after the stupid little stunt he pulled in the restroom, I wanted to show him he doesn't affect me.

At least I'm getting good at acting.

The sight of his tight butt muscles contracting with his every thrust had mesmerized me. I stood there like an idiot, gawking. I kept staring at his hips...at the tattoo of a cursive H with three dots.

Honesty.

I don't dwell on the meaning and push back the anger because, like it or not, I need him in this business, and his personal life is none of mine. But as my tour manager, he needs to stay on top of his game. And I'm a little surprised because I would have thought he'd kicked his drug habit after everything he's been through.

"Thanks." I know he's staring at me from the way his head is angled, but I can't see a damn thing behind his sunglasses. No doubt his pupils are dilated and the sun isn't helping. "I didn't think you'd want to talk to me."

I shrug in a non-committal way. "What you do is none of my business. But I don't want your problems to affect my career." I narrow my eyes at him.

"Don't act like you're perfect, princess. Not so long ago—"

"I don't need to be reminded." I shoot him a look. "And don't call me that. I kicked that habit long ago when I thought it would fuck up my dream." I'm no angel. I still drink and smoke the occasional joint, but not the hard stuff. "You know the repercussions. Yet here you are given a second chance to set your life right and you're heading down the same destructive path."

"You going to lecture me?" he asks dryly.

"Nope." I hand him a sandwich I picked up from the hospitality table. "But I'm warning you, the moment your actions affect me, I'm outta here. I don't need your shit." My voice cuts out because it hurt more than I wanted it to, seeing him fuck another girl. "I figure you're going to need a friend, because you're going to make enemies."

"So you're my friend now?"

For a moment, I don't answer. I simply watch the young girl on stage perform, absorbing her energy because mine is running low. My mixed emotions are exhausting me, and I'm now fighting an internal battle of feeling jealous and admitting that I'm attracted to him. Hell, I *like* him and I can't deny it. When I'm around Wes, I don't trust myself. Guilt hits me, admitting I have feelings for Wes, so I shore up my walls. "Only in business," I yell over the music.

"What happened back there—"

I raise my hand to stop him from talking. "I don't want to hear it." But the thought crosses my mind—did he fuck me like that?

As if reading my mind, his hand touches my shoulder. "It wasn't like that between us."

I step away. "You don't get to talk to me about this. I went home to Lena. We're good. She loves me. All I want from you is some respect."

"I do respect you. Wait. You told her?"

"Of course not. What would I say? I don't fucking remember!"

"Keep telling yourself that, baby. I know you remember some things."

"Shut the fuck up."

Wes laughs in an arrogant way. "You and I, we're the same. I know you care, otherwise you wouldn't have come and brought me this." He holds up the water bottle. When he says it out loud, my throat dries and I'm stuck for words. He takes a bite of the sandwich before speaking. "And I care about you. What happened back there, it's because I care."

"That's the most fucked-up thing I've heard." I want to scream at him. "Don't blame me because you fucked Elise. *I* only care about my career, and at this point in time, you have a hand in that so straighten yourself out."

"So that's her name."

"You're an ass."

Wes nods, acknowledging it.

"Get yourself another water so you don't end up in the hospital," I hiss. I start to walk away, but he grabs my wrist.

"We fucked, but we also made love."

I swallow the lump growing in my throat. An image of me sitting on top of Wes, naked, my head back, taking in our reflection in the hotel room's overhead mirror hits me. It's a brief memory, but I remember his words: "*You're everything I've been searching for...*" He'd spoken to me like I was fucking royalty. No one had ever treated me that way. I stiffen, remembering the way he looked at me. Not even Lena has ever looked at me like that.

Wes moves toward me, reaching for me. "Gar."

I step back. "If you really respect me, then stay the hell away from me." I don't wait for his reply. I turn on my heel to search for Xavier.

I don't get far before Wes is beside me. "You don't get to walk away from me. I saw your face. You remembered."

"Stop," I warn. I keep my stride, but he stays with me. Fuck him and his athleticism.

"This changes everything. You broke my heart not remembering, but now you do. And I know you'll remember everything if you let yourself."

I'm only walking, yet my heart is racing. I stop and turn. "You pathetic son of a bitch. Don't try to guilt-trip me. So what if I remember one tiny detail? Nothing has changed. You and I have a business relationship. Nothing more." I turn to see Xavier striding toward us.

He shoots Wes a dark look.

This time when I leave, Wes doesn't follow.

Midnight strikes but I'm no Cinderella.

After the last act, the festival performers gathered in the hotel lounge for drinks before our flight south to Florida tomorrow. I love summer, but I'm going to melt onstage in the humidity. Jacksonville, then Miami, before we head west to Dallas and then on to San Diego for the last leg of the tour.

All night I kept a wide berth of Wes, instead busying myself in conversation with members of some of the smaller, lesser-known bands, sharing our experiences in getting a break. I chatted with one of the younger guys, a drummer named River, about how we got to this point in life, even revealing some of our darkest secrets and comparing tattoos while drinking rum.

I had broken my self-imposed no-alcohol rule. But damn I needed it to take my mind off my conversation with Wes, and since I hadn't seen him in over an hour, I assumed he'd called it a night.

"Which is your favorite?" River asks, handing me another glass. I lift my arm and rotate it, revealing the words, scrolls and flowers near my shoulder.

Life flows on, within you and without you.

"That's pretty deep," River says. "What made you get it?"

"It was a time in my life when I was either going to drown or learn how to swim." I think back to when my mother kicked me out of my home and I was on the streets earning favors, performing in illegal backstreet clubs to pay my own way. "And then I got this one." I point to the words below the flowers, slightly above my elbow.

Through every dark night there is a brighter day.

"It's when I decided I really wanted this life. My dream."

"Ah, so all your quotes are about dreams and life," River says, smiling in an understanding way.

"Yeah, pretty much."

"You should've seen her at sixteen."

I jump at the sound of Wes' voice. He sits beside me, his attention fixed on River.

"Even back then she had the voice of a super-star, and it was only a matter of time before she was noticed."

I screw up my face. Wes didn't know me at sixteen. But then again, I spent many a night high...

"Her big blue eyes captured the crowd just as they do now. And when she sang, it was like a song from the heavens."

"You knew me back then?" I whisper to Wes, studying his expression.

His lips curl up, teasing me, but he doesn't answer my question. "What about you, River? Any tats have meaning?"

River's eyes flick to mine, then back to Wes. Hell, how long had Wes been listening to us?

"They all mean something, man. Too many to count."

Wes nods. I don't know where he's going with this.

"You know, Gar has a particular tattoo I'm fond of—"

I glare at him. He's mentioned his delight at the rose above my clit more than once. But his green eyes avoid my piercing gaze.

"It's close to her heart. I think what you hide from the world for your eyes only means more. Because some are like portholes."

I inhale a deep breath. He's talking about the words printed under my left breast.

Show me your soul and I'll show you my heart.

"Except for the one on my ass I got when I was tanked," River confesses.

"What is it? I don't want to see it," I add, laughing.

Wes laughs too. The sound caresses me, like the afternoon sun on a spring day.

River's face flares. His chin dips and his dark hair frames his square jaw.

"We've all got one we regret," Wes says.

"What do you regret?" I challenge him, and by the look he gives me, we both know I'm not just talking about getting inked. To my surprise, Wes points to the beautiful girl's face on his arm.

"Kara was my girlfriend in college. The tattoo is good, but it reminds me of a road I shouldn't have traveled."

"She broke your heart, or did you break hers?" My tone holds no compassion.

"I broke her heart. But she's the reason I earned my first strike with a drug suspension when we hooked up years later, so I'd say we're

even. But that's another story and one I'm not willing to share." Wes stares down at his glass. He swirls the alcohol in his glass before taking a sip.

"Back to you," I say to River, trying to lighten the conversation. Wes' confession surprises me, but the regret I see in his eyes shocks me even more.

"Well, it's not a girl but someone who I admired when I was younger. I mean, not a person, but... oh hell, it's Captain America's shield."

Wes snorts.

"Hey, that's cool," I say. "At some point in life, we all have our favorite heroes."

"Who's your hero?" Wes asks.

I squirm. I grew up without money or simple pleasures like going to the movie theater. For years I thought the world hated me because my own mother said she'd never wanted me. But I watched the movies my mom liked on our old television. She sat on the two-seater couch with her current fuck-buddy while I sat on the floor. I couldn't say how many times I'd watched *The Terminator* movie.

"C'mon, Gar. Spill." Wes cocks an eyebrow at me.

My gaze shoots from Wes to River, whose expression is eager. "I told you mine," River says.

"Linda Hamilton. I mean, Sarah Connor in *The Terminator*."

My gaze flicks nervously to Wes. He's staring at me. "Interesting. What would you sacrifice for your future?"

"Whoa. Where did that come from? I think I've already sacrificed a lot for my career." I don't want to get into so I don't say anything more.

"Sarah was all about the future. And we all do what we have to in order to get to the top." He says it as if he's a friend giving me advice. "Do you regret any of it?"

I lift my chin. "Mistakes were stepping stones to where I am now."

"And where do you want to be in a year?"

My first instinct is to say, '*to be the best DJ in LA,*' but I remain quiet. To be honest, what I want most is for the person who loves me to be proud. And if that person truly loves me, then I know I'll also be proud of myself. But I don't answer truthfully. Wes is digging, I'm afraid if he digs deep enough he'll see the real me beneath my armor. And that's something I'm not ready for. So I give him my standard response.

"I just want to make awesome raves and earn some decent bucks doing so."

Wes leans closer and whispers in my ear, "Liar."

garnet

uck.”

"What is it?" Lena asks quickly. "Did I up it too quickly for you?”

"No, babe, there's someone at the door. Give me a minute while I get rid of them. It's probably housekeeping.” I remove the vibrator slowly and switch it off before I place it on the sheets. I leave the phone on the bedside table with the speaker on. "Won't be long,” I say as I grab the luxurious white robe from a hook on the bathroom door and tie the belt around my waist.

"I'll be here.” Lena's voice echoes around the room.

Cursing to myself, I open the door. Lena and I haven't managed to use the vibrator and app on our phones since she surprised me with it when

I was home. My mouth gapes. It's not house-keeping but Wes standing there in black pants and a white button-up shirt with sleeves rolled to his elbows. My hands immediately go to my hair, and I finger brush the back. His gaze travels over me. "Did I interrupt something?"

I step forward so the door almost closes behind me, trying to block our voices from reaching into the room and in the earshot of Lena. "Yes, you did. I'm taking an important phone call."

"Really? Well, I need to talk to you before our flight this morning regarding the schedule changes in Florida. Since check-out is in"—he raises his arm and his Apple Watch comes to life—"just over an hour, now is good for me."

I roll my eyes at Wes. "Well, it's not good for me. I still need to shower."

"This won't take long, Princess."

I narrow my eyes at him. Wes knows I hate that nickname.

"And you're not the only performer I need to speak to." Wes folds his arms and his weight transfers to his heels.

I huff at him. "Fine. But keep quiet while I hang up with Lena. Not a word." I raise my finger and point at him. "Understand?"

Wes nods and follows me into the room. The mood is lost so I remain standing next to the bedside table and pick up the phone, deactivating the speaker button before putting it to my ear. "Hey babe, I'm back. It was just housekeeping." My gaze shoots to Wes momentarily. He sits on a velvet-cushioned chair opposite the bed, and my heart picks up a beat when I see him staring at the crumpled sheets. Wes settles back and folds his arms.

"Good," Lena breathes. "Now put Kenny in your pussy."

"Um..." I hesitate. "Maybe we should continue this another time."

"No way. I'm all worked up here, babe. I want to hear you come for me."

"I have to check out soon." My gaze flits to Wes. He's eyeing me, a curious expression on his face.

"Come on, Gar. It will be the last time we can do this for a while. I need to hear you moan. I miss you. Please."

Lowering my rear to the bed, I curl into a ball and whisper, "How about tonight? I'll be more relaxed tonight."

"You were relaxed five minutes ago. What changed? Is it me?" Her voice trails away.

"It's not you, it's me. I'm a little worked up about the festival."

"Then let me relieve some of your tension. Please, Gar. I need this and so do you. Put me on loud speaker and put Kenny inside of you."

How do I always manage to complicate the simplest of things? It's too late to backtrack and say Wes is in my room, as it will only cause Lena to ask more questions. Lena will recognize the difference in my voice if I don't activate speakerphone. I do so and place it back on the table next to the bed. My hand grabs for the vibrator. A playful grin crosses his face. I shush him and give him my best scowl.

"You ready, baby?" Lena says loudly.

Wes cocks a brow. "Yeah, baby," I say, but I place Kenny under my breast. I can fake this and have it over in a couple of minutes.

"I'll start slower this time."

Kenny vibrates against my chest. I close my eyes and enjoy the thrumming over my nipples, my rings tingling against my skin.

"Good?" Lena asks.

"Yeah." I don't open my eyes. I don't want to see Wes' face.

"Okay, I'm going to up it, baby. I want to hear you moan."

I move the vibrator over both my breasts and I moan so Lena can hear me. The bed dips and my eyes shoot open to find Wes beside me. He grabs for the vibrator and I hold onto it as we both tug.

Wes lifts one finger to his lips. I know he's right. I can't have Lena hearing us.

He leans down and whispers, "You forget I've seen you and tasted you. Let me help you here. Your body isn't new to me."

"Fuck off," I mouth.

Wes shakes his head.

"Is it good, baby?"

My head turns toward Lena's voice coming from the phone. "Yeah, it's good."

"You don't sound like you're into it."

Wes snares the vibrator from my fingers. I spring up and slap him.

"Ooh, slapping yourself. I like that, Gar."

Again Wes places a finger to his lips. I glare at him.

"Now I really want to hear you, Gar. I'm taking control of the tempo here."

Kenny is vibrating in Wes' hand. He places his free hand on my knee, gently opening my legs. My robe is disheveled from fighting him and I'm partly exposed to him. I shake my head.

He doesn't get to do this with me. If I'm to keep his presence a secret from Lena, then I'm going to have to insert Kenny. But Wes doesn't get to do the honor. I already feel like I'm cheating by having him here watching me.

I point to the door, but again he shakes his head.

"How's that?" Lena asks.

I all but growl at Wes and open my hand for Kenny. Wes narrows his eyes, but he hands over Kenny, now buzzing madly.

I point to the door again, but Wes only stares at me. My thoughts whirl between secretly wanting him here and feeling guilty about it.

"Gar?"

"Yeah baby, it's good." I roll away from Wes, onto my side, and open my legs. I ease Kenny inside of me and gasp immediately. Lena is wreaking havoc with the tempo and I groan as my insides light up. My G-spot swells and I'm pulled into my own bubble of pleasure, my mind solely on what's happening to my body.

"How's this?"

I call out. Desire rips through my entire body, my nerves on high alert.

"Get ready, Gar."

Fuck, she must have Kenny on the highest speed. Kenny is finding every delicious part and I squirm, gasp, roll onto my back and buck my hips while holding the vibrator between my legs. My eyes are closed, enjoying the moment, but I also don't want to see Wes' face while I'm on display like this.

"Come for me, Gar."

Another jolt hits me and I buck my hips. The sensation is wonderful, but there's no touching of bodies. No soft skin to fondle. I'm lacking the edge. Then a warm mouth caresses my breast… sucking, teasing. I sigh in relief. It's the stimulus I'm seeking. Still, I don't open my eyes.

I'm lost.

My free hand reaches for Wes' hair as he works my breast. My nipple peaks beneath his tongue.

I groan madly and Lena audibly approves. Wes' mouth finds my other breast as Lena says, "This is it, baby."

Lifting my rear off the bed, I roll my hips around and around as Kenny builds my orgasm. I open my eyes to my gown completely open. My pale skin is bared to Wes. I watch as I thrust my hips, inhibition lost as Lena controls the vibrator's intensity. My red rose stands out against my pale skin and the white bed linen.

I take in the sight of Wes so close to me. His short hair is growing out, the ends becoming lighter than the roots. His eyes are closed, but I can still make out his sharp cheekbones and jaw while he's engrossed in tasting me. Then his hand cups my breast and his mouth opens further as he sucks hard. Wes' hand darts to my clit and he places enough pressure to send me over the edge. I explode, colors flying out around me. I call out, panting, seeking the air that seems lost to the room.

I open my eyes briefly when cool air touches my skin, the absence of Wes' warm mouth immediately felt. His face is so close to mine and he's watching me. Caught in the web of lust in his heated gaze, I'm only vaguely aware of the vibrator slowing to a stop. His lips lower, then he stops. I inhale a sharp breath, acknowledging I wouldn't have stopped him if he'd kissed me.

"Beautiful, Gar," Lena says gently.

My eyes close. "Thank you," I manage.

"You're welcome," Lena says, sounding chuffed. "I'll let you come down. I'll talk to you tonight. Love you."

"Love you too," I whisper. Then she is gone.

I lie still, not yet capable of moving. Realization hits that my feelings for Wes have changed. When I open my eyes, I stare only at the white ceiling, not ready to look at him. I'm sated, and confused.

He leans over and places a gentle kiss on one breast then the other before pulling the robe together to cover me. "I'll give you some time. I'll go and speak to River about the schedule changes, then I'll come back."

Before I say anything, he's out the door.

13

wes

I couldn't stay a second longer.

My cock is ready to explode. I cuss under my breath, wanting to be the one to give her the sexual pleasure she craves. I don't care what Gar says; she needed me to get her over the edge. That damn vibrator—what did she call it? *Kenny*—didn't cut it, and fuck, now I'm jealous of Kenny.

When her girlfriend told her she loved her and Gar said the words back, I had to get out of there.

Until today, I thought it was only a physical thing I had going on with her.

Fuck.

Standing outside River's door, I knock twice.

"Wes, my man. What can I do for you?"

"I have a list of the schedule changes I need to run over with you for Florida. You got a minute?"

"Sure. We're just having some bacon, gravy and biscuits. Best hangover food ever. You want some?"

Food is the last thing my stomach needs. "No. I'm good, thanks."

Five minutes later, I'm leaving River's room and heading to band girl's room.

Elise.

I remember what Garnet had said about not making enemies. And if I have to put distance between Gar and me—because after today, I'm sure she'll push me away— then it's best I stay friends with people like Elise.

Elise frowns at me when she opens the door.

"Morning, Elise." I give her my warmest smile. "This should only take a minute."

"Heard that before." She turns away and I follow her into the room.

What the hell? I can't remember much about fucking her, but I had one hell of a boner and it was a damn good workout. "Yeah, about that. I'm sorry. Coke fucks with my head. I hope we can keep a professional relationship between us. I shouldn't have—"

"Whatever," she says quickly.

"Look, I really like you. And I think you have great talent."

Her eyes round. "You do?"

I'm not sure which one pleases her more so I run with it. "Yeah, I do. So much that we've changed the schedule in Florida and your band will play after The Perils of Life and before Garnet. We think it's a better fit, since both of you draw a crowd, and we thought having the ladies perform in time slots together would be better for fans."

Elise smiles at me and I can see her happiness at being slotted next to Gar. The truth is I want to keep River and Gar apart, the jealous prick that I am. But I have a say here and I'm damn well going to use it.

After singing more praises to Elise, I head back to Garnet's room. I knock gently.

Gar opens the door. Her blue eyes find mine. For a moment, I'm lost in her. I take in her freshly showered scent, all citrusy and delicious. Her wet hair is stuck to her face. Her gorgeous body is covered by a baggy, black T-shirt and faded blue jeans. She doesn't say anything, just opens the door wider and steps aside.

We walk a few paces and stop. She goes to sit but I start talking while I'm standing, reading off the printed schedule in my hand. I quickly go over the changes and then turn to leave.

"Wait. Is that it?"

I nod. "Yeah. Something you're not happy with?"

Garnet narrows her eyes at me. "You came into my room acting like you wanted to speak to me about something important. I asked you to leave, but you wouldn't because whatever you *had* to say held precedence over what I was doing."

"It did—then. And I did have more to say. But I've worked it out." I'm going straight to hell anyway, so what's one more lie?

"So whatever it was a half hour ago is no longer worth talking about with me?" She fists her hands and digs them into her hips.

I do my best to look nonchalant. I lift my wrist and my Apple Watch comes to life. "Check-out is in thirty minutes." I lower my arm and meet her stunned gaze. "You'd better eat breakfast. I'm sure you worked up an appetite."

"You bastard," she says, taking a step closer. "You don't get to come in here, watch me when

I'm at my most intimate, and then act like it's nothing."

"You saw what I did to Elise. And you said it yourself, it's just *business* between us."

"You fucking—"

Gar stops when I take a step closer. "All I'm asking is for you to remember that one fucking night. Then you'll understand what I'm going through," I say between clenched teeth. "Because you're killing me. You're ripping my heart out, damn it."

Gar's forehead lines and her face flares. "I am remembering," she whispers. I can hear the emotion in her voice.

"It's not enough." My fucking heart is slamming against my ribcage, trying to break free. "Not until you remember everything."

"And then what?" she whispers.

"You choose."

I don't hang around. I turn on my heel and I'm gone.

garnet

alifornia. *Yeah baby.*

I lean back and smile as the plane touches down in San Diego. One more festival, then home to LA to begin my new job working at Red Star.

I pinch myself. As much as I find it hard to believe it's happening, I deserve this opportunity and worked damn hard to get it.

Still, it's un-fucking-believable.

My gaze shoots to Wes, who stands as soon as the safety belt sign clicks off. He reaches for his bag in the overhead compartment. The way he moves, strong and controlled, stirs something foreign inside of me. I let out a long sigh because I know I can't think about him in that way.

Wes has hardly spoken to me after I made it clear that I'm not about to dump Lena. When he questioned me about the night we slept together, I told him I didn't want to remember because the guilt is playing havoc on my mind.

"What is your heart telling you to do?" he had asked me on our last night in Miami.

"My heart belongs with Lena."

I can still see the hurt in his eyes.

The truth is, I'm remembering more of the night we shared every day. And it's confusing the hell out of me. I don't want to be the person who crushes someone else's heart by being unfaithful. Because that pain sucks. Been there, done that.

I pick at my nails when a voice in my head reminds me that I'm my mother's daughter. I have her genes. Although I have a tendency to royally fuck things up, I love Lena and don't want to see her hurt. And despite these new feelings I have for Wes, I'm obligated to take care of my girl.

After retrieving his bag, Wes turns and stares down the aisle. His green eyes lock with mine. For a moment, we hold each other's gaze before he turns and talks to Hart, the lead singer of Sun Beasts and the golden boy of the tour. I reach for my phone and turn it on. While waiting for a signal, I watch Wes exchange handshakes with

Hart. Whatever. But I'm not fooling anyone but myself. I miss the attention; liked that I was number one to Wes.

My phone beeps as it comes to life. I tap out a text to Lena.

Arrived in San Diego. One more show then I'm home. Missed you xx

I drop it in my bag and wait for the other performers in the front seats to file off the plane. It's a rest day, ahead of the music festival tomorrow, and Wes wants the final day to end with a bang. I've heard other people chatting about the final night's party and the surprise Marshall Thompson has in store.

Guess I'll find out tomorrow night.

⌒

The morning of the festival, Xavier comes up to my room before breakfast, his face as red as the rose of my tattoo. I'd already showered and dressed in a tank top and denim shorts. After closing the door, I sit down at the table where my make-up is spread out and finish getting ready.

Xavier sits on the edge of the chair right beside me. "Wes has rearranged the schedule and now you're on at an earlier time. I'm not sure what's gone down between you two, but you're a star act and deserve to perform in front of the Sun Beasts before they close the festival."

I'm determined not to let anyone or anything ruin my happy mood. "You know what went down between us," I say while looking more interested in rubbing moisturizer into my freshly tanned skin.

"That was weeks ago, and until Miami he still made you one of the closing acts on the main stage. I know some of the other bands get to do the closing set, but they're on the smaller stage away from the majority of the fans."

Squirting more cream into my hands, I massage it along my arms without looking at Xavier. "It's fine. Based on Twitter and Instagram, my fans will be there. I'll just post the amended time. Then I'll mention Red Star in LA if they miss it but still want to come see me."

"At least Julia has maintained your social media profile and made regular updates." Xavier stands from the chair and paces the floor.

Julia is the publicity assistant for The Rox nightclub. After calling the club while I was in Philly to notify them of my new deal with Red Star, Julia agreed to continue looking after my social media accounts until I found someone else. "Honestly, I'm exhausted and glad tonight's the last show. I'm looking forward to going home. To hell with Wes and his games."

Xavier stills. "You're right. Go out there today and show him. When you Tweet, make sure you tell your fans you're bringing something extra to the stage."

I uncross my legs and sit forward in the chair. "And what exactly did you have in mind?"

Xavier moves to sit opposite me. His fingers tap on the table. "Wes thinks you can sing. So show him. Add another song at the end where you sing the whole damn song. If he wants this festival to go out with a bang, then that's what you're going to do."

"You're talking about the song I wrote, aren't you?"

Xavier sits back. "You want to give them a special surprise, then here's your chance."

"I haven't practiced it in months. I can't—"

"I didn't think 'can't' was part of your vocabulary." Xavier folds his arms. "I never took you for a coward."

"I'm not being a coward, I'm being realistic. It could ruin me if I sing something without rehearsing it first."

"Not if you sing from your heart like you did for me. You can do this, Gar. Do it for me." Xavier smiles, the one accompanied by puppy-dog eyes that pulls on my heartstrings.

"You're an ass. You know when you say it like that, I can't say no."

Xavier jumps up and wraps his arms around me. "Don't worry about the not-rehearsing part. I know you'll kill it."

Hundreds of fans gather in front of my stage. Performing in the daylight means I'm not blinded by the bright stage lights. I can see every one of my fans, and although it thrills me, it also scares the hell out of me.

Wes has kept his distance, not bothering to come speak to me before my act. Fine with me. Standing on the side stage behind a curtain, I walk out to the center when my name is called. I wave at the fans. They're cheering, yelling their appreciation.

I don't waste time. I hit the buttons. My hands work the deck. My hips sway, my feet tap, and I pump one arm in the air when I have everything under control. The crowd sings along. I glance out to see girls on guys' shoulders, arms waving in the air.

I play out my usual song list, and on the last number I yank off my tank top and sling it into the crowd. Then I sing, as I usually do, and the crowd screams and starts to sing along with me. My fans have heard the tracks and they know the words. I smile at them, making eye contact with a dozen or so, and my energy climbs, feeding off theirs. As I finish the song, I pump my fist in the air, then turn and smile at Xavier.

Wes is standing beside him, staring at me. Struck with nerves, I give Xavier a hesitant look. Xavier nods reassuringly without smiling. He's serious about me singing solo. I swallow hard before turning back and adjusting the microphone.

"Thank you, San Diego." I shoot the crowd the peace sign. "Today, I want to give you something special. A song I've never performed live." The buzzing of excitement falls quiet.

I turn to Xavier, but he appears to be arguing with Wes. Both men's arms are crossed, their bodies angled slightly toward the other.

Fuck.

I clear my throat. "Be gentle with me, San Diego. This is a first for me, and we all remember what our firsts are like..."

The crowd laughs in unison and I smile back at them, sharing the joke. My fingers start on the synthesizer and I press the button for back-up drums from my deck. Staring into the crowd, I sing to them. Words flow deep from within my heart, and as I hit each note, tears form. They burn my eyes but don't fall, each word touching a sacred place buried inside of me.

Like an animal trapped, I lived in a cage
Starved and barely alive, I dreamed of liberty
One rainy day someone forgot about me
And during a storm, I managed to set myself free
The streets were my home, strangers my friends
With my heart numb to love, you helped me
I stole from you, hated myself so I hated you
And then when I trusted you, you left me
My heart knew nothing else
I was nothing, not worth it
And just when I thought about ending it all
You saved me.
You didn't give me diamonds or offer me your bed
You taught me how to use my time, because it's all I had
Time waits for no one,
And the world doesn't care for my dream
But you taught me that I matter
As bad as it all seems
With every new day, the sun will rise

Dark nights will see brighter skies
You saved me
And if given a chance to change things
I'd do it all again
I couldn't risk not meeting you so
I'd do it all the same

I turn as my fingers play out the final sounds. Xavier is staring at me, eyes rounded. I can't help but notice that Wes is no longer by his side. Shaking Wes from my thoughts, I turn back to the crowd and sing:

You saved me.

As I hold the last note, I raise my hand in the air and point to the crowd. When I stop, the roar of appreciation is deafening. A smile splits my lips as sheer joy bubbles up inside of me. The hairs on the back of my neck prickle and my skin tingles like never before, seeing and hearing the way the crowd responds to me.

"Thank you, San Diego." I blow kisses and turn off my mic before walking to the side of the stage and straight into Xavier's arms. He squeezes me and lifts my feet off the ground. "Don't ever tell me you can't sing. That was friggin' awesome. Expect Twitter to explode," he says and grins.

"Wait." I pull out his phone from his pocket and run back on stage.

Stopping in the center, I switch on the mic. "For the memories," I tell the crowd. Then I turn and take a selfie, trying to get as many fans behind in the shot as possible. "Here's to my awesome manager." I wave Xavier out on the stage. The crowd is still cheering. I take another selfie with Xavier and the adoring mass of people behind us. "For Instagram," I tell him. We both wave to the fans as we walk from the stage.

The stage crew rushes out to disassemble my deck. "Be careful with my baby," I tell them.

Xavier yanks a clean tank top out of his bag and throws it at me. I pull it over my head and then we walk down the stairs together, ready to celebrate. As we head to the VIP area, I'm playing on Xavier's phone, loading the photos to social media. The 'likes' already adding up.

"You know, Wes did me a favor slotting me in an earlier time. Now I have longer to celebrate." I laugh, as I zoom in on one of the images. Wes is in the photo, standing at the front of the crowd. And the way he's staring at me, it takes my breath away.

garnet

alfway through the evening, I turn off all my social media notifications. My phone is permanently lit up like a Christmas tree. Now's the time to party, not be distracted by my phone.

Lena has called me twice. The first time after my performance was posted. Apparently, she showed every customer who came into her boutique. The second call came after dinner. She sounded excited that her own Twitter and Instagram accounts had registered ten thousand new followers. Guess fans were stalking my photos and put two and two together.

Unlike Lena, I wasn't excited about that. Both Xavier and I agree I need to be more careful with what I post. My life is now under scrutiny and any wrong turn could upset fans, which could be costly. Until today, I'd never felt like a fucking insect under a microscope. I may have signed up for this, but Lena didn't. And I hope she can handle the hype.

Really, it's not the fans I fear but the trolls, although trolls are not something I want to think about tonight. I'm riding this wave and enjoying the high while it lasts. Every performer is here at the party and it's been one hell of a celebration, complete with exotic dancers performing for us. It's been nice to sit back, relax, and watch for a change.

Marshall Thompson made a brief appearance earlier in the evening, followed by a grand exit after the belly dancers' act. Come to think of it, I haven't seen Wes since then either.

The entertainment has come to a close, and I'm both tired and elated. After downing the last of my gin and tonic, River offers to order me another. I wave my hand at him. "I think I'll call it a night."

He glances at his watch, and I know exactly what he's going to say so I stop him before he tries to talk me out of it. "Before you say anything, I need to stay focused. After I fly back to

LA in the morning, I have a meeting at Red Star in the afternoon." I smile at him.

River high-fives me. "Stay in touch, Gar." Then we hug.

"When are you heading back to Chicago?"

"Day after tomorrow." He grins at me, and Elise snuggles in under his arm.

Cute.

Inside the elevator, I text Xavier. It's a little after midnight, but he often watches television until late.

You'll be happy to know I'm heading to bed now.

I add an emoji of a princess crown and laugh as I hit 'send.'

Walking down the long hallway, I pass Wes' room. I stop and listen. Nothing. My intention is to keep walking.

I knock lightly.

After a few seconds, I turn to walk away... he's probably asleep. But as I do, the door opens and Wes is standing there, shirtless, in jeans with the top button undone.

My mouth goes dry perusing his hard, muscled frame.

He reaches up and touches the top of the doorway, resting his body on the wooden frame.

"Gar." His tone drips with acid. "Something wrong?"

I shake my head and say the first thing that comes to mind. "I missed you tonight." What the fuck? That came out wrong.

"Really? Last I checked you were having a great time. By the way, congratulations on your performance today."

I nod once, a million questions storming my mind. Instead of embarrassing myself more, I go with, "What time did you leave?"

"Around nine-thirty."

"Oh." It didn't fit that he preferred being alone in his room to partying. "Is something wrong? Did you get into a fight with Xavier?"

He laughs once in a sarcastic way, and I'm a little embarrassed I assumed his bad mood was because of me. "Not Xavier, Marshall."

"Really?"

"Yeah. And I'm not going to discuss it with you out here." He folds his arms and doesn't say anything. I can't help but notice the way his biceps bulge and his chest muscles flex.

"Do you want to talk about it?" I say, almost a whisper.

"To you?" His dry tone cuts deep.

"I'm a good listener."

Wes stares at me a moment, then he nods. "Fine." He steps aside and opens the door for me.

Inside his room, I take in his belongings hanging neatly in the closet. The door is left open as though he's packing. Everything is folded perfectly, not at all like my clothes.

"You want a drink? Coffee?" He opens the bar fridge.

"A water would be great. Thanks."

He hands me a bottle of water before he flops onto the bed, linking his fingers behind his head so his beautifully sculpted abs are on full display. I stand a moment and look for somewhere to sit.

"There's plenty of room on the bed, Gar. I don't bite."

I shoot him a look before settling at the opposite end near his feet. I sit cross-legged, facing him. "So what did you and Marshall fight about?"

"Many things. Rumors. My role when we return. Trust. My personal life."

I snort. "Your personal life is hardly his business. Who does he think he is, your father?" I say in a mocking tone.

Wes gives me a long look. "Marshall *is* my father."

I struggle to mask my shock. "Is that why you work for him?"

"Only way to keep my ass out of prison."

Under the influence of alcohol, I slowly comprehend his words. "He's controlling you?"

Wes laughs, yet there is no humor in the sound. He rubs his hands over his face. I crawl closer and touch his arm. "He doesn't really control who you are. You only have to do enough to keep him happy, but he can't influence your life."

Wes stares up at me. His green eyes are wide and vulnerable. "You don't know him like I do. Marshall can control anyone he comes in contact with."

My head whirls. "You let him sign me." I stare at Wes. "You know what he's like, yet you convinced me to sign."

"What can I say, I'm a bastard." His eyes lower, avoiding my line of sight.

I think of everything Wes has said to me... the way he looks at me. In my heart, I know he wouldn't simply hand me over to the devil. I lean over and force him to look at me. "I know you. If you thought I was signing my life away, you would've stopped me. Right?"

Wes only stares at me. His hands rest on his chest. "I signed you because it was best for your career. You'll make it under Marshall. But I was also being selfish. I wanted to work with you. I wanted you around me." His voice is quiet and controlled, and I blink, trying to grasp his words.

I'd told Wes I'm a good listener, but I need to know more, especially if I'm to work for Marshall Thompson long after the tour. Easing onto my elbow, I stretch out alongside him. "So when did you find out he was your father?"

Wes twists to face me. "I've always known." His gaze lowers as his fingers pick at the bed linen.

"He raised you?" I cringe at my tone.

Wes shakes his head. His gaze fixes on a spot on the bed, then his eyes glaze. "He left when I was a toddler. He made yearly visits and paid my bills. My mother met someone else, Stan, and married him a short time later. He was nice enough, but he treated me as though I was the neighbor's kid overstaying my welcome."

"Well, I know what that's like. I didn't know my father, but my mother treated me like a pet that somebody gave her and she never wanted. At sixteen, I worked up the courage to move out."

Wes nods and I get the impression he knows part of my story. "Your song. Some of it was about your mother?"

"Yeah. The beginning where I compare my life to living in a cage."

Wes remains quiet a while, as though absorbing my words. "May I ask who the other person is in the song? The one who saved you?" I glance away. Wes' hand covers mine.

I'm staring at the ink on his fingers. "It's not who you think."

"I know you love Lena," he says and my eyes find his. "But I assume there were many before her."

"Not many... that I loved anyways." His Adam's apple bobs in his throat. His eyes flick across my face and I'm surprised to see uncertainty behind them. "I've loved three people. A girl before Lena, and a guy before her." I study his expression before continuing. "It took a while for me to trust anyone. But the song's not about them. I wrote it for a homeless man. I can still see his face after all these years. Thomas looked out for me for six months. He really did save me."

Wes lifts a finger and tucks a wayward strand of hair behind my ear. "You're something else, you know that?"

I snort lightly, and yet his compliment warms me.

"Have you kept in contact with your mom?"

I shake my head. "You?"

"Yeah. My mom and Stan live in St. Louis. Marshall splits his time between LA and San Francisco. I'm planning on remaining in LA. So... I'm now homeless. Do you think you could write a song for me?"

I slap his arm. But somehow I can't help smiling, knowing we'll be in the same city.

His green eyes meet mine with new warmth, but then he looks somber once again. "I seriously don't know where I belong." His tone is flat. "After growing up in St. Louis, I played college football in Texas, then moved to San Francisco to play in the NFL. I have a couple of homes, but none I *call* home. Have you ever wondered where you fit? Where you belong?"

"All the time."

He studies my face and I can tell he's hesitant to ask me something. "What?"

"Did you really consider... you know... what you said in your song?"

"Ending it all?"

Wes nods once, slowly.

"Yeah. I considered it because I struggled to see my worth, to see beyond the pain, physically and emotionally."

"You're an amazing lady, Gar. And I'm glad you reconsidered."

"You and me both. Part of me wanted to prove her wrong, you know?"

Wes stretches and kisses my forehead. "Stay with me tonight?" he whispers. "Just to sleep, I swear."

I search his eyes, looking for lies. Instead, I find raw honesty, and for a brief moment I see fear before he shuts it down.

"I don't want to be alone," he continues. "Nighttime sucks when you're alone and under attack by your darkest thoughts. When you close your eyes, you have no defense. There's no left tackle to protect me in my sleep." He smiles half-heartedly.

I nod, understanding that better than anyone.

wes

don't wake her because I simply want to look, and take in Gar's beautiful face. Looking is not breaking the rules. I shift my weight on my elbow, and although I'm close, I don't touch.

Gar is sleeping in the same clothes she wore last night, a skimpy sapphire top and tight black pants. Even with her eyes closed, I know the color of her shirt will accentuate her eyes. Along her delicate arms, I trace the outline of her tattoos with my eyes, ingraining every detail into my brain. What I'd give now to see the ink under her breast and the rose above her sweet pussy.

It's a little after eight, and I know I should alert her to the time but I'm selfish. I vaguely remember waking a few times during the night.

Gar's scent, the warmth of her body lying beside mine, reassured me of the trust we're building, and I settled quickly, placing my arm around her waist and snuggling in behind her.

It was the first decent sleep I've had in months.

So whoever is banging on my door at this time of the morning clearly didn't sleep as well as me. I cuss under my breath and slowly get up so I don't disturb Garnet. When I jerk open the door, I'm surprised to see Marshall, dressed in his standard black suit. I run a hand over my head. "Morning, Marshall."

"Wesley," he says curtly. "Not a good one I presume if you're still here." He folds his arms and angles his chin so his nose points down. Fuck, I want to wipe that arrogant look off his face. "You should be in the restaurant with the artists, considering some have earlier flights. Not everyone is flying home to LA."

"I'll be down in half an hour. I have a few things to attend to first. Besides, I thanked everyone last night and said my goodbyes at the party. After the heavy celebrations, I assumed most wouldn't be up for a while."

Marshall's gaze shifts over my shoulder and I step sideways to block his view. But I know I'm too late when a smirk grows on his face. "Garnet. Quite a surprise."

I turn to see Gar standing behind me. Her hair is ruffled and she's wearing the same clothes as last night.

I glare at Marshall. He assesses me. I know that look. "So already you've chosen not to take my advice and mix business with... pleasure."

"It's not what you think—"

He dismisses me. "Meet me in my office in LA at three. I have another flight to catch at seven tonight."

"You're heading back to San Fran tonight?"

Marshall nods once. "Three o'clock. Don't be late."

After closing the door, I apologize to Gar.

"It's not your fault he's an ass." She smiles at me. "How did you sleep?"

"The best in months."

Garnet's eyes lower as though she's guilty of something. "Me too." She fidgets a moment. "Well, I'd better get back to my room and finish packing. Not that it will take me long 'cause I just throw everything in. Unlike you," she says, waving her hands at my closet. "Plus, I still need to shower and probably eat breakfast."

I take a step closer and place my hand on her shoulder to stop her rambling. "Thank you. I really appreciate you staying the night."

Her blue eyes meet mine, and neither of us move or speak. "I'd better get going. I'll see you..."

"Maybe at breakfast." I smile at her and then she strides to the door. She shoots one final look over her shoulder before the door closes behind her.

It's not a coincidence I'm sitting next to Gar on the plane. After arriving early at the airport, I arranged it when I checked in. We hardly speak at first, but as soon as the plane is in the air, I notice Garnet biting her nails.

"Do you want to talk?" I ask before she secures her headphones.

She frowns at me. "Talk about what?"

I close my iPad and stick it in the seat pocket in front of me. "Anything to take your mind off the flight."

Her chin dips. "That obvious?"

"Why didn't you say something at the beginning of the tour?"

Gar shrugs. "I didn't want to look weak."

"After your performance yesterday and what you told me last night, weak is the last thing that comes to mind."

She almost smiles. "Not everyone is what they seem."

"You're right, they're not." At this moment I wish Gar knew me better. "Look, I know parents can be... *frustrating,* but it's good to know your roots, to make peace with yourself. And I was thinking about your dad. Do you know his name?" Her expression hardens so I concentrate on keeping my face calm.

Her gaze lowers, but I can see her walls building. "No, and I don't want to. He never bothered with me, so he and my mother can both go to hell." Her tone is stiff, yet she keeps her voice soft so only I can hear.

"Do you think it would help if you met him? Let go some of the anger?"

"Why are you bringing this up?" she says, almost snarling. "I thought you wanted to take my mind off flying?"

"It's exactly what I'm doing." I give her an easy smile.

"Not sure what's worse," she grumbles.

I laugh quietly. "Okay, new subject. What do you feel most grateful for in your life?"

Her head tilts. "Easy. My music. You?"

I glance down to her fingers, still tight around the armrest. "Being alive." She stares at me, but before she speaks, I add, "Sometimes I partied so fucking hard, I thought I wouldn't wake up."

Gar nods. "Yeah. Sometimes I don't know how I got through the partying days."

"Do you ever think about how you'll die?" Gar's eyes widen. "And it won't be on this plane." I smile reassuringly before continuing. "Some nights I lie awake thinking of all the times I could have died... and most would have been my own fault. I like to think I'll die of natural causes, you know? Of old age and not by my own doing. Though at this rate, my body will give up sooner than I'd like."

Gar shrugs. "I like partying, but sometimes it gets dull. Like it's wearing thin. Some nights I wake up with the worst pain in my gut and I know I should ease up. Then I get scared and think about how I should go on some health kick or some crazy-ass diet. But the next night I'm feeling okay and just fall back into old habits."

I make a sound as though I understand. "We should both go on a health kick for a month. Eat healthy, follow a diet, and exercise regularly. We could check in and see how the other is doing?" Despite being in good shape, I'm not as fit as I used to be, and I'd do anything to remain in Garnet's life.

"Maybe," she whispers and glances up at me with uncertainty. I know she's thinking about Lena.

"I want to be your friend." I don't smile, so she'll know how serious I am. She glances down to her lap but doesn't respond. "So tell me, what do you value the most in a friendship?"

Her head falls back against the headrest and she makes an exasperated sound. "I value someone who can take my mind off flying."

"Very funny. Seriously, I want to know."

Gar picks at her nails. "Respect is definitely at the top of my list and trust is also a big thing for me, even though I've messed up myself."

I want to tell her that she wouldn't have messed it up if Lena was the right person for her, but I keep my mouth shut. She's opening up to me and I fucking love it.

She's still picking at her nails so I assume her thoughts are making her nervous. "Loyalty. Friends have to have your back even if you fuck up," she says.

I place my hand over hers. "I think that stands for friends and lovers."

She angles her head slightly my way and glances up at me. "Not if it's your lover you screwed over." Slowly, she removes her hand from mine.

"But screwing someone over doesn't just happen. If you slip up, it's because there are already problems between the two of you." When she looks at me as though I don't understand, I add, "And I'm not talking about what happened between us. That's complicated." Fuck, I've killed my point.

"It's complicated now that I'm remembering more," she whispers.

My heart flutters and I smile. I can't help it. Her remembering us together is a step toward her feeling differently about me.

"It doesn't change anything."

I scratch my forehead. "I know." But it's a start. If she could only remember the words she told me, I know things would change between us.

The plane has started its descent, and Gar inhales sharply when we hit some turbulence. "Hey." I touch her hand, and this time she links her fingers with mine. "Here's another distraction. We stare into each other's eyes for two minutes. You don't speak. Only focus on the eyes. After two minutes, we will have landed." I raise my other arm and let go of her hand to set the timer on my watch.

"I don't think—"

"Go." I stare into her blue eyes and take control. Gar blinks rapidly, uncertain. Her eyes widen with every bump. I find her hand and lightly squeeze, my gaze unwavering. I take in their beauty. Her dark lashes fan her almond-shaped eyes. The white of her sclera is clear, as though she's rested. I want to smile, knowing I had a part in that. The blue of her iris is perfect and I discover navy flecks among the lighter blue. Her pupils dilate a little, and I sense her looking deeper... searching.

I keep calm and remind myself that this is not about me and my fear of what she'll see behind my mask. It's about Garnet, helping her to overcome her fear of flying.

Garnet blinks, her trance-like expression transforming to one of awareness as the plane slows along the runway. "Thank you," she whispers.

"You're welcome," I say sincerely, then force myself to look away.

Damn, I can't help wanting her.

17

garnet

I close my eyes and tilt my head back onto the pillow when Lena takes my breast in her mouth. Her hand goes to my jeans. "Menses?"

"What?" I murmur. My eyes flash open. "Oh, I um... I never got it." My thoughts whirl. "Too much stress and flying must have messed with my rhythm."

"Yeah, probably." Lena pulls my jeans down my thighs, along with my thong. "I've missed you." She feather kisses her way to my rose. "And your meeting at Red Star went well? When do you start?"

I don't want to think about work. Only her touch. "Yeah. Saturday."

She lifts her head. "Tomorrow?"

I nod quickly then I stroke my breast, not wanting to lose the mood.

"Great. I'll get the gang to come watch."

"I, um—" I don't finish saying I'd rather not have the gang there on my first night when I'll be full of nerves because Lena's mouth is making my body sing. Her tongue teases my clit and I squirm with pleasure. It's been too long and I'm writhing inside with need. She inserts two fingers and fucks me, then three, while her mouth sucks on my clit. I'm building. My hands caress my breasts, tugging lightly on the rings, and I moan, desire building within me.

Lena stops and crawls beside me, her fingers still inside my pussy. She changes her angle, and her lips close over mine. I'm tasting her and tasting myself. It's a total turn-on. I open my legs wider. Her fingers pump into me faster. Then I moan into her mouth as I come. There are no bright colors exploding around me, but still it's wonderful. And I'm happy to be home.

⃀

My first night at Red Star and I was the opening act for BountEE, the most popular DJ in LA. My gig finished around eleven and he took over when the real party started.

From the third level I look down, watching him pump out the vibe, seeing the energy he brings to the club. Part of me is jealous and the other part in awe. But I can't help thinking, *fuck him and his professional dancers on stage.*

The whole place is electric. I look away from the lights to steady my emotion. Lena is chatting with Peta. Yeah, she called the whole gang and they're all here. Lena laughs, and I don't miss how overly friendly she is to Peta. I'm not in a talkative mood, so like a moth drawn to the light, my attention is lured back to the stage.

Disappointment fills me that I was only the opening act. I understood when I signed that I'd be the main artist. I guess if it weren't a Saturday, I probably would be. Hell, I had a great reaction from the crowd tonight, and thanks to Twitter and Instagram, my fans showed up in masses. And at least I got to sit in the VIP lounge.

Sweaty bodies grind out moves on the dance floor in sync to the vibes. After making a promise to myself that I'll soon be the number one DJ, I head outside to the upstairs balcony and look out toward the dark ocean. The lights of Third Street Promenade twinkle not far away. Getting a gig in Santa Monica is a dream, and I have to remind myself to be patient. I just need to prove to Marshall I'm a good investment.

"You did great tonight."

I spin around at the sound of Wes' voice, surprised yet not surprised that he's here.

"Rather be on the stage now." I turn my back to the ocean and lean on the balustrade.

Wes doesn't say anything but leans his weight against the rail and looks out to the sea. He's wearing his usual black suit and white shirt.

"Will I always be the opening act here?"

His gaze remains fixed on the ocean. "Marshall wants only the best. He wants you to learn from the best."

I fold my arms across my chest. "My act is unique."

"Most DJs are in some way or another. He must like you, otherwise he wouldn't have signed you. But I'm not here to discuss business. Your little text had my head spinning, and I want to know the meaning behind it."

Oh fuck.

I forgot I sent him a text last night when I couldn't sleep. I'm no longer worried since I bought a pregnancy test this morning and it came back negative. I didn't think I was pregnant, but it was one extra concern playing at the back of my mind and I needed to eliminate it. God knows it's been years since I've had to stress about birth control.

I glance over my shoulder to make sure we don't have an audience before answering. "I'm late so I took a pregnancy test, but it's all good."

Wes stiffens. His lips part, but he says nothing for a moment. "Yet you *thought* you were... why didn't you mention it earlier?"

"I was trying not to dwell on it, since I figured it was the stress of flying along with the performances that put my body out of whack."

Wes' expression changes and he looks at me as though I just spoke to him in another language. "Right," he drawls. He continues to stare, as though he's waiting for more of an explanation. But there's nothing more I want to say. Not here at least. He runs a hand over his head. "It's been a long day, so I'm going to go. See you around, Gar." Leaning forward, he kisses my cheek.

I still as his warm lips brush my face, his scent jolting my memory. Before I say anything further, he walks away and I'm staring at his back as he heads toward the door.

As I come out of my trance, I see Lena standing at the door, eyes wide. She walks over to me and stops a good two feet away. "So you and Wes... you're close?"

I shrug. "He was just telling me about my next gig." I can't believe how easily the lie rolls off my tongue.

"By kissing your cheek?"

I look at the door and then back at Lena. "He's teasing me because he knows he doesn't affect me. Because I'm with you."

"It didn't look that way from where I was standing."

I take her hand. "He means nothing to me. I love you." I pull her into my arms. My shoulders relax when her hands tighten around my lower back. "Let's go home."

Lena takes a step back. "I'm not sure where I call home anymore."

"What? With me, of course."

"No, Gar. Things are changing between us. We're both changing."

"Nothing's changed," I say in a louder voice.

Lena closes her eyes a moment before opening them. "When were you going to tell me?"

Panic starts to swell inside of me, hearing her tone. "Tell you what?"

"I'm not stupid. I just worked it out after seeing you with Wes. I didn't believe it at first—"

"There is nothing going on between us," I say, my voice full of desperation.

Lena's eyes flick over my face. "I saw the pregnancy test in the trash can."

I swallow... hard. "I can explain."

"I don't think I want you to. But I need to know, does it have anything to do with Wes?"

My throat burns as the panic in my gut rises. I know I need to be honest, so I choke out a response, "It was a mistake. I was drunk."

Lena closes her eyes. "Not again." When she opens them this time, I'm surprised to see that she's perfectly calm. "I should be angry, upset... but I'm not. It hurts a lot, but I think I knew a while ago it was the beginning of the end. It kills me that you cheated on me—again. I'm even more surprised it's a guy. And to think you acted like you never liked Wes." She snorts. "You need to stop lying and sort yourself out. Work out what and whom it is you want. It's not me. We both know that."

"You're wrong—"

"I don't want to be with you anymore. I think I knew it while you were away. I love you. But I'm not *in* love with you. I love being with you, and I love all of this." She waves her hand, implying the club. "I guess I haven't been honest with you either. So you're free to go, to do whatever— or whoever, as the case may be."

My eyes burn with tears at how easily she's dismissing me. I'm in shock and struggling to find the words. "I don't want to be free. I want you."

"No, you don't. Can't you see it? It's been an amazing three years, but we owe it to each other to move on and find ourselves. You'll always be special to me, but I'm letting you go." She lifts onto her toes and I think she's going to kiss me. Instead her lips touch the corner of my mouth. I squeeze her hand, wanting her to stay. "I'll come and get my things in the morning."

"You're not coming home with me tonight?" Of course she isn't, but I'm desperate.

"I'll stay at Peta's." She releases my hand and walks away.

I scrub my hands over my face before grabbing hold of the railing to balance myself. Squeezing my eyes shut, more tears fall to my cheeks. My stomach is in knots and I can't find any oxygen, even in the cool night air. It's my fault. I could've done more to hang onto her. I know Wes is the icing on the cake but not the only reason. Lena said so herself. She started feeling this way a while ago.

Fuck! I'm just like my septic mother. My arms wrap around my body, and I think of the quickest way to ease the pain. My fingers swipe away the tears and I head for the bar. The pain of being not wanted hits me like a wrecking ball. Old wounds open and I only know one way to heal them.

After downing a few rounds of shots, I head outside to find a cab. I don't check to see if Lena and my friends are still inside. After unlocking my phone, I send a message to Wes.

Where are you?

Home. Why?

Which is?
What am I doing?

Pacific Coast Highway, Malibu. Do you want the number? If you do, then I'll assume you're coming for a visit.

Assume away.

wes

Sitting in a chair by the door, I'm waiting like the fool that I am. With one hand, I unbutton my shirt so it's not so tight around my neck. My phone provides a distraction as I scroll through Instagram searching #Redstar #Garnet. I smile at all the posts. Girl has got herself a decent fan base. I switch to Twitter and use the same hashtags. Before I read any posts, my phone is vibrating in my hand and I jump out of my seat.

Fuck, Gar has me all jittery and it started with that damn text she sent last night. I'm still confused what to think. At first I was nervous, then anticipation took over.

What is the code?

Instead of sending her the code, I unlock the back door, open it, and then press the remote to my garage door. As soon as it starts to open, I hear the cars on the Pacific Highway. I hate being so close to the traffic, but at least I have the ocean outside my front door.

After a moment, Gar's jeaned legs come into view, then her black top. I smile and lean on the doorframe. When the door raises enough for me to see her face and how blotchy her skin is, I push forward. "Everything okay?" I ask as I walk between my Yamaha motorcycle and my black Porsche.

She doesn't move. Her gaze flicks to both my wheels. Her chin dips and her fair hair spills forward, screening her face. Her chest heaves and I realize she's crying.

"Gar." I walk to her and wrap my arms around her tiny frame, pulling her close to my chest. It feels good to hold her.

"It's over." She sobs a little. "It's me. I destroy everything I touch."

"You don't." I kiss her hair. "From my perspective, everything you touch turns to gold."

Gar's arms tighten around my waist. "I'm just like my mother."

My heart swells, knowing how upset she is and yet she trusts me enough to come here to talk about it. Slowly, I guide her away from the garage door and hit the remote so it closes. "I assume you don't want to talk out here, so shall we go inside?"

Gar nods her head against my chest. She pulls back and I lead her inside to my lounge area that overlooks the ocean. It's dark out and you can't see anything, but the French doors open to the balcony and you can hear the waves crashing against the shoreline, which at this time of night are almost under the house.

Gar stiffens as she peruses the room, taking in the furnishings. "Take a seat," I say.

"I don't want to sit. Can you give me something to help take my mind off all the shit that's going on in my head?"

"What were you thinking? A cup of coffee? Because I'm not giving you anything hard. You have another gig in a couple of days and the last thing you need is to fall into a coma of self-pity and drugs."

Her hand swipes at her cheek. "I can't stand the pain. It's eating me up."

I walk to her, take her face in my hands and kiss her forehead. "It doesn't last."

"It does when you're the cause of it."

"When you tell yourself something over and over, you start to believe it. There are two people in a relationship and two people break up. The responsibility never lies with one."

"Since when are you an expert on relationships? How many have you been in?"

My lips tighten. I know she's hurting, but lashing out at me won't help. With the back of my hand, I run my fingers down her cheek. "I've been in three. Two in college, one in my second year of playing NFL."

"And how long ago was that?"

"Six years ago. Did you come here to discuss my love life?"

Gar snorts. "Your love life. I thought you only fucked."

I close the distance between us. "How much have you had to drink?"

"Why?"

"Because you always shoot your mouth off when you've been drinking."

"I'm not drunk."

I arch one eyebrow. "I believe it because you're still feeling the pain."

Gar closes her eyes for a moment and nods. "I thought some cocaine would help."

"Is that why you came?"

Her eyes flicker to mine and I see the guilt. "It's not the only reason. I thought you'd help me to forget."

I give her a long look and fold my arms. "By fucking you senseless?"

"No. Yes. I don't know," she whimpers.

Over the past month I've gotten to know her, know damn well that she's not weak. But I feel useless in helping her. I'm not gong to be the guy that fucks her and then she forgets.

Not crossing that bridge again.

It's not that I don't want to, because I do... more than anything. But the next time will be different. "I won't touch you. But I can return the favor and stay with you for the night. Trust me, it helps. What you need is sleep... and my room has a great view in the morning."

"No fucking then?"

I give her an easy smile. "Not tonight."

wes

Daylight burns through my eyelids. I didn't close the damn curtains. My arm moves to touch Gar and the bed is empty. I turn toward the light to find Gar standing on the balcony in nothing but her black bra and thong. My lips twitch and so does my cock. Her ass is a fucking awesome sight in the morning.

I must have groaned because she turns, then strolls back into the bedroom.

"Morning." Her eyes travel down my body. She smiles at my noticeable hard-on under the sheets. "Do you want a hand with that?"

I hold her gaze. "I don't joke about sex."

"Neither do I." She scoots closer then sits on the edge next to me. "I've had time to think. Work out why I really came here." She runs a finger along the length of my cock. "And you said no fucking last night." I grab her wrist. "It's a new day, and I'm not drunk."

"Your heart might be broken, but mine's not. I'm not going to rush into anything." Her fingers wrap around my cock.

Fuck, I want this more than anything.

"Who said anything about rushing?"

I let go of her wrist and she pulls back the sheet. I watch her carefully as she takes in my body. Her appreciative expression relaxes me. Gar strokes the length of my dick then she lowers her face and opens her lips.

The heat of her mouth sends pleasure straight to my core. She sucks hard, sliding me in and out, her tongue flicking and circling while her hand gently cups and squeezes my balls. I don't want to come right now so I try to think of anything other than Gar's soft lips around my dick. My hands tangle in her hair and I buck my hips. She gags a little but doesn't stop. Fuck, I feel like I'm fourteen. "I'm gonna come, Gar." I need to tell her in case she wants to stop. I know Gar's been with guys, but she was with Lena for three years, preferred girls even before her, and I don't want to push her boundaries before she's ready.

She sucks a little harder as her hand squeezes my balls. I come in her mouth, my hips thrusting once as I do. Through hooded lids, I watch her face as she swallows quickly before releasing me. I'm panting and rubbing her shoulder, not capable of much more for a minute or so. Gar sits up and grins at my satisfied expression.

"Like getting back on a bike."

I cock an eyebrow. "Really? Well, I hope you like marathons."

She lowers her lips to mine and before they lock, she whispers, "If you remember anything about that night, you'd know marathons are my specialty."

I grab her shoulders and hold her still, my gaze pinning her.

She smiles coyly.

I loosen my hold so she can kiss me. Then I flip over. Gar's under me, and I kiss her hard and long. "What do you like?" I say against her lips. "Tell me what you want."

"Everything we did that night."

"Works for me." My hand snakes around her back and snaps open her bra clasp.

"Quite a skill, Mister Black," she purrs as I toss it aside.

I chuckle, but my attention goes to her full breasts. I could honestly say I'm in love with them. My mouth finds her nipple and I suck while my fingers tweak the other. I lick, suck, and lightly tug her ring with my teeth. Gar groans under me and it's the green light I'm waiting for, so I give the other breast equal attention before trailing feather kisses to her navel... to her rose.

I lick the rose stem right down to the flower. Her hips twist and I plant my hands on her to keep her still.

Sliding my body further down, I push her thighs apart. I stare into her eyes as my finger slides along her folds. Her gaze holds mine, her lips slightly parted as she breathes at a quicker rate. I push two fingers inside and find that she's already wet. Gar groans and I smile at her easy pleasure. I pull my fingers out and suck on them. Garnet's eyes remain on me, but she says nothing. Then I reinsert three fingers, pushing deeper... faster. Gar writhes on the bed. My mouth replaces my hand while I fuck her with my tongue.

"Wes," she says with urgency.

I gently suck on her clit. Gar's thigh is shaking under my grip and she's breathing so fucking hard. I insert four fingers and curl them to find her special spot. With my other hand, I press on her clit and then sit up so I can watch her face when she comes.

Gar's hands slam down on the bed twice as she calls out my name, along with God's and the whole trinity. I don't stop. My fingers start to cramp, but I rub harder inside of her. She exhales so loudly it's almost a scream. Garnet closes her eyes and then her expression softens. Her body falls limp as she sinks into the mattress. One hand lifts as though she's surrendering. I grin and ease my fingers out of her, sucking them again, needing to taste that sweet orgasm.

Lying beside her, I kiss her shoulder and stroke her face while she regains control. "You okay?"

She chuckles like only she gets the joke. Without looking at me, she says, "It's so much better sober."

"Yeah, it is, baby." I run my fingers over her breasts. "It doesn't matter who you're with, it always feels better when you're sober. Especially if you respect the other person."

Her eyes flick to mine. I don't mean to make her uneasy, but I have a need to express myself, and fuck, I've never felt like I needed to before. Except with Gar. She turns everything around and upside down. She spins me round. Now I'm giddy and not sure what I believe anymore. But I believe in her... in us.

"Whether you're with a girl or a guy, your heart will know why because of who that person is inside, not because they're a certain gender. You respect them for who they are, not what they are. We're all the same, baby. Regardless of the color of our skin, gay or straight. It doesn't matter. It's in here that counts." I thump my chest lightly. "You respect the person who lives in the body. Fuck, I'm rambling."

Flopping back on the bed, I cover my eyes with my forearm. I sounded like a complete fuckwit. I suck at being... whatever it is I'm trying to be. "I'll give you a minute." I jump up and head to the bathroom to take a quick shower, a colder one than usual because I need to calm my raging cock.

I'm only gone a few minutes, but when I walk out, Gar's no longer in my bed. I wrap a towel around my waist and head into the kitchen. She's standing by the counter wearing my white shirt that I wore last night.

She turns and smiles. "Coffee?"

My gaze follows the buttons of the shirt, the edge of the material gaping so her breasts are partially on show. I look lower and suck in a breath. The rose on her mound peeks through, and my cock lengthens under my towel.

I nod once. My insides tighten, and I'm not sure if it's the sight of Gar in nothing but my shirt or the fact she is here in my kitchen looking quite at home. When she turns to the espresso machine, I walk up behind her and wrap my arms around her front, pushing my hard-on into her back.

"Excited for coffee, are we?" She laughs lightly and wiggles her butt against me.

I spin her around, push the mugs and sugar out of the way, then hoist her up on the island. Standing between her legs, I kiss her neck before nibbling on her ear. Sliding the shirt over her shoulders, I kiss her breasts, her navel, her rose. Her gentle sighs spur me on.

I lean to the third drawer and pull it open and find a packet of condoms. I rip open the packet with my teeth, and with one hand I release the towel, all while my eyes are fixed on Gar. She is on the counter watching me, her legs wide—waiting—and I'm trying to get the fucking condom on my cock quicker than the rubber will roll. Hooking my arms under her thighs, I angle her pussy toward my cock. Her hand grabs my dick and she circles her entrance first. "It fits," I remind her and smile. Gar laughs lightly, then her heels dig into my butt and she slides herself onto me. I push a little and stop when she gasps.

Her eyes flame, watching my face, and it makes me fucking nervous. I know I need to be gentle with her, but my male instinct is telling me to plunge into her and fuck her ass hard.

"If I remember right, a perfect fit," she whispers.

Her words undo me, and I push all the way in. Gar cries out, and I hook my hands around her ass and pull her closer. I'm lost in the warmth of her pussy sheathing my cock, her muscles clenching around me. Gar's breathing is as rapid as mine. Her eyes become glassy and I know she's about to orgasm. "Not yet, Princess." I part her butt cheeks and thrust deeper. My gaze lowers, distracted by her tits bouncing up and down as I ride her sweet ass. Her strength weakens and she falls back so that she's lying flat on the granite. I take in the sight of her and ingrain it into my brain... her thighs looped over my arms, my hands on her butt, her tits bouncing in front of me. I hiss and focus on the tattoo under her left breast:

Show me your soul and I'll show you my heart.

Her hand touches her breast and she moans under her caress. Watching her nipple peak, I rock into her harder. I let go of her thigh and find her clit, applying pressure with my thumb. She calls out and I reach for her head, supporting her behind the neck so I can watch her beautiful eyes glaze over. I fist my hands in her hair and curse as my orgasm builds deep in my gut. Inhaling sharply, I thrust deep and shudder with the release. I exhale loudly, my entire body zinging in pleasure. I still, then curl over Gar, my rapid heartbeat threatening to break free. Her breast pillows my head and I listen to her strong heart until it quiets and our breaths slow.

Garnet's fingers caress my hair, making little circles. Tilting my head sideways, I peer up at her, not ready to move my head from her chest. I'm enjoying the sound of her steady heartbeat, and my cock is extremely happy to remain inside of her. But I need to ask. "Did I hurt you?"

I see her smile. "Do I appear to be in pain?"

I chuckle low and nuzzle her breast. Gar lifts her thighs and circles them around my back, the angle perfect. My dick reacts. "You want to go again?"

"I'd like to be able to walk out of here," she jokes, yet I can hear apprehension in her voice.

"Not if I can help it," I say, my voice sounding huskier than I intended.

She slaps my shoulder. "For that, you can make me coffee."

"And then I'm going to have you again," I warn.

I wink, and slowly move away. I can't wait to take charge in the bedroom.

garnet

arshall Thompson called Wes around midday and said to be in his office for a meeting by two. I feel sorry for Wes being Marshall's puppet, but then when I think about it, Marshall controls all our strings. Still, he has a firmer hand over Wes and I know how Wes hates being controlled.

After Wes left, I headed outside to sit on the balcony and take in the ocean view. Until now, I'd ignored my phone messages and used the memory of Wes and me together to block the hurt of Lena from my thoughts.

With Wes no longer here to take my mind off it all, my walls crumble and I'm feeling the sting of the knife twisting away in my gut. Inhaling the fresh, salt-bathed air, I gather my courage to call Lena and ask how she's doing.

I've had time to think about Lena and me. There's no doubt I loved her—I still do—but I have a desire to nurture and take care of something and not be like my mother. Our relationship had become more like best friends, with the addition of sex. Best girlfriends with benefits. Not having her in my life is like having a fight with my best friend, and now we're not talking. But I know we'll make up because we're close. At least I hope we do.

The way Lena acted last night... she wasn't pissed, more resolved. She even admitted she saw it coming a while back. Nonetheless, it still hurts. We loved each other despite growing apart.

Plopping my feet up on an outdoor lounge, I glance at the notifications on my screen before unlocking it. One in particular catches my eye. Swiping my phone, I open up Twitter.

Breanna Butler @Breanna_Butler

@LenaVHeusen She's a bitch. You don't need her in your life. Proud of you #djgarsucks #redstar

"What. The Fuck."

I scroll down.

My feed is full of hate posts.

I sift through long conversations. Then I see the original post from Lena, bagging me for breaking up with her and blaming Wes for the split.

Fuck!

Switching to Instagram, the posts from supposed fans are all the same. Oh shit, except there's an image someone has taken from last night of Wes kissing my cheek on the balcony.

#makeupyourmind #fake #cheater #redstar

More pictures of Lena crying with my alleged friends.

#Garbrokemyheart #fake #cheater

This is crazy.

I press the button to call Lena, my heart racing as I wait for her to pick up.

"Hello, Gar," she says, her voice dripping with contempt.

"Lena. I was about to call you and check to see how you are, but then I saw all the posts and I'm confused—"

"Damn right you are. You've humiliated me. Seems like your fans weren't all about you. You've upset them."

"I'm not calling you about my fans. I wanted to see how you were. Last night, you acted like you were cool about breaking up with me. Yet you've posted all this other shit and made what we had public."

"Of course it's public. I was in a relationship with a famous DJ. One who was a lesbian and dumped me for a guy. You have no idea what you've done to me."

I can hardly believe what I'm hearing. "You instigated the break-up."

"*After* you slept with Wes and thought you were pregnant. Fuck you, Gar. You're a bitch."

"Yeah, I guess I am. But this is between you and me, not my fans and not the whole fucking world. And why are you hash-tagging Red Star? Do you want to get me fired?" I suck in a quick breath. "That's it, isn't it? You're trying to get revenge, and you want my ass fired from my dream job."

"You don't deserve to get what you want and I get nothing. Besides, you don't even like all the clothes those fashion houses send you."

My mouth gapes—I'm lost for words. Lena didn't stay with me for me. She loved my life-style, my fans, the publicity, and being spoiled with the latest fashion. "They wanted to see their clothes on me, not you. Deal with it."

"Fuck you."

My fingers rub at my temple. "Lena. We're better than this. We loved each other. Please, can we keep this between us?"

"You apologize for humiliating me, and then we'll talk."

"I'm sorry, Lena. I told you that already. I never meant for any of this to happen. I'm surprised and confused."

"I don't mean *now*. I want you to Tweet your apology."

"Are you kidding? I can't understand why you want this to be a public break-up. Do you want people to take sides?" I choke out.

"Yeah, I do. Let your fans decide whom they support, me or you." I wince at the caustic tone in her voice.

I stand up and pace. "I don't even know you..."

"Oh, that's the pot calling the kettle black."

"That's something your mom would say."

"Yeah. She was right about you. At least I have a mom who cares."

"What?" I whimper.

"Deal with it."

"What do you want? Money? I don't want us to be like this."

"I want nothing. I'm fine on my own and I have the support of your fans to prove it."

"Okay," I croak. "I'm going to hang up. We'll talk when you've calmed down." I turn to see Wes walking through the living room toward the balcony. He drops his suit jacket over the couch. Tears pool and spill onto my cheeks, and it hits me how much I need him.

"Whatever," Lena says, then she's gone.

I stare at my blank screen a moment longer before looking up at Wes. He strolls over to me, wiping his thumb over my cheek.

"Lena hates me," I sob. "She's turned this into a social media war."

"I know," he whispers.

"She's trying to turn my fans against me—wait. You know?"

"Unfortunately, yes, and so does Marshall." His voice is low and his tone makes me even more nervous.

"Fuck. Am I fired?" I fail at keeping my voice calm.

"No, baby. But he's making me move back to San Fran. I'm supposed to be gone by the end of the week."

"What? No." I throw my arms around him.

Wes kisses the top of my head. "Marshall believes that if I leave, everything will simmer down. He told me trouble always follows me."

"That's not true, and I don't want you to leave." I bury my head into his chest, realizing at this moment how much I need him in my life.

"I don't want to leave you." His hands rest on my shoulders. "I want to ask you something, but I don't want you to answer straightaway. Think about it. But I promise you, I mean every word." He pauses and waits for me to nod before he continues. "I want you to come with me to San Francisco. It could be a fresh start for both of us."

Staring into his beautiful green eyes, I see Wes in a different light. Yes, he's the guy who has fucked up. We both have. But it's obvious he's trying to make amends, and who am I to hold his past against him? Plus, we are good together despite how little time we've actually spent in each other's arms. Sometimes you just know, and although I've tried to deny it, there has always been something about Wes that has drawn me to him. Maybe it's fate.

I step away from him, afraid...confused. I made a promise to myself years ago that my work would always come first. So how do I give up the dream job I've worked so hard to achieve?

"I can't," I manage to say.

Wes kisses my forehead. "You can do anything if your heart wants it."

garnet

iss you x

The four a.m. text message from Wes tugs at my heart. I just finished working my first gig as the headlining DJ at Red Star, where I rocked everyone well into Monday. For two weeks I've been the sidekick act, but tonight I owned the stage.

Miss you too xx

I want to say more—much more—in the message, but I don't. Instead, I hold back, fingers quivering over the keypad on my cell.

After refusing a ride home with Xavier, I sling my bag over my shoulder and walk along Third Promenade. I don't know where I'm walking. All I know is that I don't want to go home... alone.

It's only been two weeks since Wes left for San Fran, and I could never have anticipated how much I'd miss him. Damn Marshall-fucking-Thompson to hell for being right. After Wes left, I received hundreds of messages on social media. My fans assumed I was single and heartbroken for Lena. Those that had flocked to her have since migrated back to me, offering their sympathy. Now they want the two of us to reconcile because we were "so good together."

Not a fucking chance.

Turning the corner, I head toward the beach and decide to call a cab and crash at Wes' Malibu home. I've stayed there more times than my Venice Beach apartment, just so I can feel his presence... smell his scent on his pillow.

Heard you ripped it up tonight.

I smile at Wes' text.

Yeah, I did. Why are you awake?

Winding up the last act now. You'd love it here, baby.

I visualize Wes working with the DJs at Red Star in San Fran, and I can't help but feel a little jealous.

You know Marshall won't allow it.

My chest burns. The high of performing dissipates as reality engulfs me that I'm now another one of Marshall's puppets.

I need to call Wes so his voice can wrap around me like a warm blanket. I don't dwell on why I need him when I feel unsafe or unsure, I just hit the call button.

"Hey. You okay?"

Simple words, yet I close my eyes briefly and imagine he's beside me, encasing me in his arms. "Yeah. I'm about to catch a cab back to your beach house. I don't want to go home."

"Come." His words are soft but there's a tone to his voice like he's commanding, not asking.

"You know I can't. We have to ride this through and see what happens."

"I just got you, and I hate not being with you. I want to see you," Wes says in a strained voice. "I want you in my bed."

I stiffen, hearing the firmness in his last words. "We need to take this slow," I say softly.

"Why? Because you don't want a rebound relationship? I'm not accepting that as a reason, and like I told you before, I'm happy to be your rebound guy."

"It's not... an excuse. I just think we need to slow it down and get to know each other better. I want us to last."

There's a pause before he responds. "I've been thinking about that. You consider a rebound as going from one relationship to the next to avoid the pain of a breakup?"

I nod, although he can't see me. There are still so many emotions coursing through me. The pain of losing Lena—my lover and best girlfriend— and then the anger of her betrayal. Add to that the hollow ache in my heart and then top it off with the pain in my gut of not having Wes by my side. My feelings for him are strong, but I need to challenge us... determine whether we are meant to be together.

I swallow before answering. "Yeah. Because people see rebound relationships as emotional neediness and assume they won't last."

Wes chuckles lightly. "Fuck other people. You can be as needy as all hell with me. I know I fucking need you. I'm not your substitute. In fact, I see it in a whole different light. Like a basketball player."

"I have no idea what you're talking about."

"A rebound is one of the most important fundamental skills of basketball, Gar."

I snort. "Don't patronize me. I know what a rebound is."

"Just hear me out. A rebound can determine whether a team wins or loses a game. When a team is down and their player shoots and misses in the last seconds of a game, if their team gains an offensive rebound, then they have another shot at winning. If a defensive player snares the rebound, then they've lost their chance. In the same scenario, if a team is up by a couple of points and they shoot the ball and miss, then they hope one of their own players gets the rebound. If the defensive team gets the rebound and there's time left on the clock for them to score, then it's game over. You get what I'm saying?"

I close my eyes momentarily. Not really. "You want to be my rebound guy."

"No. I want to be the only guy who rebounds. I want every possible chance to prove myself to you. I'm not allowing any other bastard in on a rebound opportunity. It's me and only me, and I want to win."

"It's not a game, Wes," I say softly.

"No? Love is a game, Gar. Everyone takes a risk of getting hurt."

I hate it when he talks this way. "I don't see it like that." A cab pulls up on the other side of the road and I wave. "I have to go. We'll talk tomorrow, okay?"

"I'm going to talk to Marshall—"

"Don't," I warn. "Let me handle it my way."

"He won't fucking listen to you." I sigh, hearing the frustration in his voice.

"Then I'll make him listen. I have a weekend off in two weeks. I'll come there and you can show me around."

Wes makes a sound like he's defeated. "Okay. Two weeks."

2 2

garnet

ome.

I've been putting off coming back here for days.

Lately, I've snuck in to crash when it's dark or just popped in to grab more of my belongings to take to Wes' place. I *feel* too much here. I feel Lena even though all of her shit is gone, including the television and the ugly cat statue that sat near the front door. She took the majority of the clothes sent to me by the fashion houses too. It didn't bother me except for one black tank top. It had low-cut armholes and a frenzy of color on the front. I liked it because the design was different. It was a beautiful mess, and Lena knew I was attached to it.

Speaking of a beautiful mess... I'm so over thinking *Fuck you, Lena*. I don't want to feel resentment or anger because it indicates I'm still attached to her, even if it's in a negative way. And in my mind, those negative emotions point to a rebound relationship destined for disaster.

My legs turn to mush. I sit on the couch and rub my hands over my face as though it will erase my thoughts—and the past. I stare into the doorway of our bedroom.

My bedroom.

I force myself to stand because I need to locate my cell and call Xavier before I change my mind.

"Gar? Everything okay?"

"Yeah. Hey, I want to sell my apartment. Can you hook me up with a realtor?"

There's a slight pause before he answers. "Is this a rash decision or have you thought it through?"

"It may be rash, but I can't stay here. It's fucking killing me being here, even for a few minutes."

"Moving won't solve all your problems."

"Yeah, well I think it will. I'm staying at Wes' beach house for now. I'll stay there until I decide where I want to live."

Xavier is silent for a few moments. "There's a party tonight. Claire is celebrating her promotion." I snort. Claire has taken my previous DJ position at The Rox. "Come. Have fun. It would look good for you to be seen there. Show you've moved up in the world and with no hard feelings toward her."

"I like Claire."

"Then what's stopping you? You don't think you're better than your old coworkers, do you?"

I cringe at his words. "Fuck off. You know that's not my style."

"So I'll pick you up around nine? Oh, and stay at your house. I'm not going all the way to Malibu then back to Ladera Heights."

Xavier arrives in a stretch limousine just after nine. I shoot out the front door, not wanting to stay a moment longer in my damn apartment.

The driver opens the door and I step inside to see Xavier holding up a glass of whiskey on the rocks. The ice tinkles as he circles the glass in his hand before I take it from him.

The strange woman sitting beside Xavier surprises me. Her arm is looped through his like they know each other well, and yet I've never seen her before. Usually when I see Xavier, we chat about business and my personal life. Guilt slaps me in the face at how selfish I've been not to ask about his.

"Gar, this is my girlfriend, Chelle."

"Girlfriend," I repeat slowly. Chelle shifts in her seat. "Sorry, I didn't know." I stare at her a moment and take in her pretty features. Dark, wavy hair falls over her shoulders. She has alluring, almond-shaped brown eyes and high cheekbones. "Nice to meet you, Chelle," I finally say and hold out my hand.

Her eyes flutter before her gaze meets mine, and damn, I get why Xavier is attracted to her. She takes my hand and shakes it lightly. "Nice to meet you, Gar. Xavier has told me so much about you."

"All good, I hope." I let go of Chelle's hand, noticing the full-length navy dress she has on. I look over at Xavier and see that he's wearing a suit. Suddenly, I feel underdressed in my black denim jeans and red, strappy top. "Just where is this party?"

"A friend's house."

"Is there a dress code?"

"Yeah, but there was no point telling you because you'd wear whatever you like anyway."

I smile at him. "Anything else I should know?"

Xavier waits until I down another shot before mentioning that my old friends will be at the party since they are now friends with Claire. It takes me a minute to comprehend he's talking about Lena. My chest tightens as the car veers toward the curb. "And you know Lena is with Peta, right?"

No, I fucking didn't. I stare at him. "Why did you bring me here?" It takes all my strength not to lose my shit in front of his new *girlfriend*.

"For closure. So you can move on. You know I'll have your back." He takes my hand as we exit the limo, and then he reaches back and helps Chelle from the car.

My mouth falls opens. I'm not Xavier's priority tonight. And being a third wheel was not how I imagined myself when I next saw Lena.

"You two can talk if Wes isn't here. It would only add fuel to the fire if he'd come with you."

"Who said I wanted to talk?"

"I think you do. You were friends first, and I know you miss her friendship."

My gaze lowers and I curse under my breath. "Lead the way, Deepak Chopra."

We are met by security at the entrance before Xavier leads us into the triple-level home. Some of the faces I recognize as we weave through the crowd toward the back, where a marquee covers the gardens. Lights twinkle in the surrounding tree branches and I tilt my head to take it all in.

Noticing more partygoers spilling onto the balcony on the second level, I ask, "Who did you say owned this joint?"

"Claire's cousin. He's fresh out of college and signed with the Texas Rangers, so she's taking care of this place for him. Drinks, ladies? What will it be?"

"I'm happy with whiskey." I turn away to check out the crowd and see Claire chatting with a group of guys all wearing caps. I didn't recognize her at first, since her black hair is now cut short at the nape of her neck. I make my way over and smile. Like me, Claire is wearing black jeans, which she's paired with a black leather jacket that has more buckles than I can count. Claire catches sight of me before I reach her and she opens her arms. My shoulders relax at her welcoming gesture. "Hey, congrats, girl." I hug her tightly.

"Thanks. It means a lot you being here," she says genuinely. "I was hoping Xavier would bring you along, but I thought you might have a gig."

I shrug my shoulders. "Night off. But I worked the stage last night." We knock fists. "Enough about me, how's it going for you? Can't believe I'm missing the ol' joint."

"It's pretty damn cool, ya know. I'm getting a decent crowd every night and I get to play some of my new raves. Everyone's hitting them, which is fucking brilliant. Didn't know how'd they react to my style being different from yours."

I push my fingertips into the tight front pocket of my jeans. "Whatevs. You're a cool chick. I knew they'd love you."

Claire jerks her thumb toward some guys standing nearby whom I didn't notice until now. "Have you met my cousin's friends from college?" White teeth appear even whiter against their dark skin. I nod, but before I can get acquainted, Xavier calls out to me. I excuse myself and head back to Xavier and Chelle.

"Lena is watching you closely from the balcony." He hands me a whiskey. "Don't make it obvious," he adds quickly, stopping me from turning in said direction. "I think it's time you have that chat."

I start to tell him that now is not a good time, but I honestly don't know when a good time would be. So I down my drink before winding my way through the crowd and into the house. I quickly climb the stairs and find a bathroom to hide in while I consider what I'm going to say. Reaching for my cell that's tucked in my bra, I call Wes.

"Hey baby, I was just going to call you. I have a surprise."

"Me too," I say quickly. "I'm at a damn party for Claire, which Xavier thought was a brilliant idea for me to attend, and Lena's here with Peta. 'Cause apparently now they're friends and all with Claire." I'm breathing heavy, fighting back a lump the size of an orange growing in my throat. I'm waiting for Wes to say something, but he doesn't. Panic sets in. I don't want him to think I can't handle myself around Lena. "It's a pretty cool party though. Some dude's house who plays baseball. He's Claire's cousin. The raves are okay. Did I tell you Xavier has a girlfriend?"

"Gar."

"What?"

"Where's the party?"

"Ladera Heights. Don't know the street. Anyway, I'm not staying."

"Relax. Enjoy yourself. I'll call you soon and see how you're doing. Keep your cell close."

When he ends the call, I step out of the bathroom, but I'm not sure which way to go. Do I remain upstairs and talk to Lena, or go back and tell Xavier to have his own damn conversation with her. I know I should find Lena and act like an adult, but the thought of things turning hostile makes me want to run away and head straight down the stairs where I came from. Before I make a decision, Peta is in my face and hugging me.

"Missed you, girl. Where you been hiding?" She then holds on to my arms and looks over me as though she's assessing my health.

"Just been busy. I'm putting together a new mix with new sounds." It's only when I take a step back that she frees my arms. "How are you?" I didn't need to add *"and Lena"* as her eyes glaze over with guilt.

"Good. The whole gang's good. We miss you."

I nod and look to my cell when it buzzes in my hand. I've never been so grateful to get a text from Xavier:

Why the fuck did Wes want to know the party address?

For a split second I'm annoyed at Wes for checking up on me, but then my thoughts are back to Peta. Before we can awkwardly attempt any further small talk, Lena appears next to Peta and curls herself into her side. My insides clench remembering how she used to latch on to me whenever we were out, like she needed bloody protection. Now I think it's an act, as though she wants to appear needy. Whatever it is, her mannerisms piss me off.

I nod my head as if we hardly know each other. "Lena."

"Gar," she purrs like she has a secret. She lifts onto her toes and whispers in Peta's ear while both her hands remain clinging to Peta's arm. It's only now that I notice Peta is wearing one of the designer dresses that was sent to me, and Lena is wearing a long gown from an Australian fashion house. I grit my teeth and watch Peta excuse herself so that we can have a few moments alone. Then Lena takes my hand and walks me to the corner of the balcony.

"Plan on throwing me over?" I scowl, letting go of her hand.

"I don't hate you. In fact, I wanted to tell you that I miss you."

Her soft words shock me and I turn to see if Peta is around to hear her. The balcony is full of strangers, but that doesn't mean they don't know me.

"I've missed you too." The words fall from my lips so quickly I surprise myself. "I've missed our friendship. Our chats. Just being ourselves." A longing inside of me surfaces, and I reach out to hug her in a quick gesture. "I really want us to remain friends."

"I want that too," she says and smiles.

When I let go of her, I glance away, not wanting to look into her blue eyes, afraid of what I'll see. My gaze darts down to the marquee, and I catch sight of Xavier and Chelle before they disappear inside. When my eyes find Lena's, she's studying me.

"Xavier has a girlfriend." She smiles warmly, yet her tone holds no surprise.

The thought that she already knew throws me off-kilter for a second, but I push it to the back of my mind. "Yeah, about time." She laughs and my gut reacts. "I'm glad you're happy. All I've ever wanted was for you to be happy."

She takes my hand again and steps closer. "And you? Are you still with Wes?"

I nod, but my gaze darts downward. "Yeah. We're taking things slow. I want to establish my spot at Red Star and he needs to be in San Fran."

I shrug. "Not a lot we can do about that for now."

"Your work has always come first... surely he knows that." My eyes find hers and briefly I sense anger behind them.

"He does. My music is all I've ever known. It's what gets me through the dark times."

Why the fuck am I saying stuff she already knows?

Lena fidgets and her brow pinches. "What about the good times, Gar? Why do you push hard then? Because honestly, sometimes you push so hard you drive those who love you away." Her thumb skims over the skin near my wrist. "You need to find another outlet besides just your music." I'm surprised at how calm Lena's voice is, so all I do is nod. This is what I've missed. "You need to be happy, and not just making raves."

She reaches up and her fingers brush my cheek. Before I realize it, her hand is behind my neck and our lips are touching. It's a gentle kiss...slow, with no urgency. Her lips are soft and full, and it's practically second nature to kiss her back. Her fruity perfume engulfs my senses, and my thoughts whirl.

But then *she* breaks the kiss. I stare at her, not fully comprehending what the fuck just happened. All I know is that I liked it... and that's what bothers me the most. But not as much as kissing Wes, and not enough to risk what I have with him.

In that moment of recognition, I take a small step back. Her head tilts to the side and she grins like she knows something I have no clue about. Her gaze darts over my shoulder. "It doesn't make us even, but that kiss told me what I needed to know."

I'm gawking at Lena like an idiot, and when I finally come out of my haze, she's already pushing past me. I spin around to find Wes leaning on the wall behind me, arms folded, green eyes drilling straight into me.

wes

Watching Garnet kiss Lena rips my fucking heart out. I trusted her, even though I knew she still had feelings for her ex. I didn't expect her to stop loving Lena, but being *in love* is different and I thought Gar was in love with me. The only thing that stopped me from walking out of this party was seeing Gar's arms by her sides. Not once did she reach up and touch Lena. Yeah, it fucking hurt, but seeing how she wasn't into the kiss as much as Lena, it may well have been a peace offering. 'Cause that's how Gar ticks.

She turns and stares at me, her blues eyes round and full of panic.

"Surprise," I say unenthusiastically. It's all I've got since I didn't tell her what my surprise was over the phone. But I've lost the excitement in my voice that was there only minutes earlier. Gar doesn't say anything. Her pretty face pales. "Not the welcoming I was hoping for..." I stall, but she doesn't even bat a lash. "Do you want to explain that?"

"I don't think I can." Her voice fades away. "I don't know what the hell just happened."

"I could tell." I move away from the wall and closer to her. "You didn't even touch her."

Gar blinks rapidly. "No, I didn't, did I?"

"You want to talk about it?" I step a little closer. Out the corner of my eye, I notice some guys paying attention to me and hear my name being whispered. I'm not in the mood to talk football. Until a moment ago, I had one thing on my mind and that was getting Garnet Delaware into my bed.

"I'm sorry," she finally whispers. Her gaze shoots down. "I'm not sure what the fuck is wrong with me."

I need her alone so I grab her hand and lead her down the stairs, keeping hold of her hand so she stays with me. "We're going to my place. You okay with that?"

"I didn't even want to come here," she says, now sounding stronger.

"I asked my driver to wait out front." I stop at the base of the stairs near the entrance, because I can't wait a minute more. "I need to ask you something. What did Lena say to you to make you want to kiss her?"

Gar shakes her head. "I don't know... I miss her. She was my best friend and I miss that. We were chatting and I really believed we were going to be friends again. Before I knew it, she was kissing me." I nod, knowing she's still hurting inside. When we step out onto the sidewalk, she says, "I miss her. And I liked kissing her."

I push my fingers through my hair and spin away. "Not what I want to hear, Gar," I snap as I search for my driver.

"I know. But I need to be honest with you. I miss kissing her, but I miss kissing you more. And I want to be with you more. I just don't want to fight with her, and I don't want to fight with you either."

"Good." I pull her against my body. "Because I'm not going to fight with you. I'm going to fuck you and remind you how much you've missed me." Taking her face in my hands, I kiss her—hard. I don't want to hear anything more about Lena.

I release her as my driver pulls up beside us. As I open the door, I say, *"Dixi"* and start to step inside, but then I hear Gar gasp behind me.

"What did you just say?" she whispers.

With one leg inside the car, I freeze. Slowly, I turn back to her. *"Dixi."* Gar's lips part. Her eyes round, yet she doesn't say anything. "It's Latin for—"

"I have spoken," we say together.

"I know what it means," she whispers. "I've only heard it once before... when I was sixteen."

My breath hitches. I said it to Gar nine years ago after she'd performed at a dodgy nightclub. I remember the night well. It was the night she doubted herself—doubted her entire life—and I'd said things to shake her up. She was beautiful. Dirty, but beautiful. A raw, young talent still untarnished by the industry. She was doing some illegal stuff and hating on herself, but she knew where she wanted to be—and that wasn't on the streets. She wanted the stage, the bright lights, and the adoring fans.

I promised myself back then I'd help her. Even slipped her boss some money so he'd keep her on for a while until she found her own way. I can still see her innocent face as she performed on the stage, her big eyes nervously scanning the crowd. But then she'd stared into the bright lights and her eyes twinkled as her voice carried all of us away.

That night I knew there was something special about her... my heart raced watching her, listening to her, and at the slightest touch of her skin. Yet I pushed those feelings away and thought only about helping her to fulfill the dream at her fingertips. All she needed was a lucky break. And for once, the arrogant college football jock could do something for a chick who needed me for something other than my cock and to say that they'd slept with the quarterback.

Garnet didn't know me. All she knew was that I was with a group of college guys on vacation. I was visiting my father in LA because he'd demanded it once a year, since he was paying for some of my living expenses. As usual, Marshall was too busy to spend quality time with me, and therefore he never found out about the late nights I'd kept in LA. I couldn't go to the popular clubs and risk being seen, so I frequented the illegal clubs in back alleys.

And that's when I saw Gar. Considering I'd recently split with my girlfriend who was the definition of fake, meeting Gar was like feeling warm sunshine on your face after months of wintery gray skies and icy winds. She wanted nothing from me, and everything about her was real. Gar filled the emptiness in my gut; she was the very thing I was searching for.

But I knew I couldn't go after her while I was in my third year of college. I had too much at stake... and she was only sixteen. So I made a vow to find her again and kept an ear to the ground listening out for her name on the club scene. With each visit to LA, I got to see her perform... got my fix of Garnet Delaware. Even if she didn't know it, I was there watching her from the sidelines and keeping tabs on her career.

I snap back to the present to see Gar in front of me, still standing and staring. Marshall had insisted I take Latin classes in college—which I hated—yet when I'm with Gar, the words flow freely. So I say the quote by Seneca, which I'd also said to her that night. *"Non est ad astra mollis e terris villa."*

Gar shakes her head disbelievingly, then whispers, "There's no easy way from the earth to the stars..." She tilts her head. "A guy with blonde dreadlocks said those words to me a long time ago. I remember him. He had the most"—

Gar steps away and shakes her head again—"mesmerizing green eyes."

I open my hand to her. "Yeah... looking back, it wasn't the best decision to grow my hair." Gar takes my hand as we step inside the car. I keep hold of her hand, afraid she'll want to run.

She continues to stare at me as though I'm a ghost that has returned to haunt her. "I never thought I'd see you again."

I signal the driver to take us home before turning back to Gar. "Why?"

"You... you said things to help me, and I promised myself if I ever saw you again, I'd thank you. Pay you back because I know you slipped money to that scumbag, Stefan."

"I did." I'm embarrassed she knew about that, so I glance down to her hand firmly between mine. "I was always around. I kept an eye out for you. Watched you bloom."

"But your name... it was—"

"Marley?" I smirk at her. "Some dumbass in college called me Marley because of my dreads, and unfortunately it stuck." I curse under my breath. Gar's beautiful face frowns, taking it all in.

"We didn't have sex that night," she says so softly I barely hear her.

"No, we didn't."

"But we could have. We were making out. I remember."

I scratch my jaw. "I remember wanting to. But you got high and I wasn't going to take advantage of you."

She blinks and her expression changes. "You said something else to me, before I got high."

I'm honestly surprised that she remembers all of this. Every moment is ingrained in my memory, but I didn't think I'd made an impact on her like she did on me.

"You were, er, kissing my boobs. You made me feel really good." I grin at her but say nothing so she'll continue. "Your fingers circled my nipple and then made invisible lines over my heart. You said, '*perfer et obdura; dolor hic tibi proderit olim.*'"

Ovid. My hand skims her cheek before slipping behind her neck. I lower my head, watching her eyes, and before our lips touch, I whisper, "Be patient and tough; someday this pain will be useful to you."

And then I kiss her, and we don't stop kissing until the car stops.

Wasting little time, I head straight to my bedroom upstairs, withholding the urge to take two steps at a time since Gar's hand is locked secure-ly in mine. She follows me in silence, keeping up with my pace. I curse under my breath when an image of Gar kissing Lena pops back into my head. I'm jealous as all fuck as I open the door to my room. I let go of her and stride toward the balcony, pulling off my shirt and throwing it aside. Using more force than necessary I pull the curtains apart before unlocking the glass and ce-dar doors to the balcony. The salty ocean breeze hits my senses and I inhale deeply. I sense Gar standing in my room, watching me. It only takes a moment for me to gather my wits and say, "Come and stand with me."

The warmth of her body touches my back be-fore her hands wrap around my abs. Her lips brush my shoulder and I close my eyes, savoring her touch. I feel her kiss the tribal tattoo on my shoulder before she presses her cheek to my skin.

"Deep down, I knew," she whispers. "From that first night at The Rox when I looked into your eyes, I knew. I couldn't put my finger on it, but there was something about your eyes that drew me to a safe place. I didn't like feeling that way since I was with Lena, so I blocked you out. I wanted to hate you for confusing my thoughts while I was with someone else. But I should have listened to my gut when it was telling me something." She looks up. "I'm sorry."

I turn and wrap my arms around her and kiss her tenderly. I walk her backward until we bump into the bed. I continue to kiss her neck as I slide her top over her head and unlatch her bra with one hand, tossing it aside. My mouth finds her breasts and I suck and nibble, tugging playfully on her rings. She groans softly. My cock reacts, straining against the material of my pants. Dropping to my knees, I slide her jeans down, along with her panties, and push her gently so she lands on the bed.

"Lift your feet." I remove her shoes before sliding the tight denim over each foot. "Wait here." I disappear momentarily to find a belt and necktie from my closet. When I walk out, her gaze locks onto my erection. I can't help but smile seeing a twinkle in her eye. Stopping directly in front of Gar, my cock throbs close to her face. She reaches up to touch it, but I grab her hand and stop her. "Move to the middle of the bed." Her eyes flicker to mine, but I'm staring at her with my best poker face.

She does what I say, then I tie her wrists to the bedposts. Her eyes seek mine, and I sense her apprehension. "Trust me," I say in a calmer tone. "You'll enjoy this." I hear her exhale, but I don't stop because my damn cock wants to explode and I intend to pleasure her first.

Starting at her elbow, I kiss the outline of her tattoos, making my way to her shoulders, down her sternum, bypassing her beautiful breasts to the tattoo underneath her left breast. I lick the words, curling my tongue as though I'm imprinting her heart with the meaning. I glance up and give her one last look before positioning myself between her legs and planting a kiss on her rose.

2 4

garnet

is lips feel like electricity, shooting sparks beneath my skin. My head is giddy with memories of the guy I've been waiting to return to me. I never believed in fairy tales or believed there was a Prince-fucking-Charming out there for me, yet here I am with the man who turned my life around. The man who disappeared and I never thought I'd see him again. To think I once despised him, and now...

When Wes' tongue caresses my pussy, I close my eyes, my back sinking further into the mattress. I groan, and my legs widen with every lick. Desire builds, overriding the emotion of secretly loving Wes as a hero for the past nine years. Yet here he is, worshipping my body when I should be the one adoring his warrior body. With an urge to grab hold of his hair while his face is between my legs, I pull against the restraints. The sound of the creaking posts breaks the seal of his lips from my pussy. I gasp in disappointment.

Wes pushes up onto his hands, his tattooed arms corded with muscles that contract with the tiniest movement. Our gazes lock. His darkens. "I tied you up because I'm going to watch you come without the distraction of your hands all over me. But as soon as I untie you, there'll be no holding back."

On command, my body responds to him, but it's more than lust and sexual desire. Right at this moment, I realize it's about me. It has always been about me. Comprehending the truth excites and fulfills me. It takes me less than a second to figure out I'm in love with Wes.

I always have been.

Wes is not my rebound guy.

My back arches as heat soars through me with every flick of his tongue.

"Wes," I moan when his fingers dive inside of me. He finger-fucks me hard, and I'm bucking my hips while pulling hard against the restraints.

"That's it, baby. Come for me, Gar."

Desire is building and building, but I want Wes inside of me to finish me completely. Lift-

ing my head, I meet his determined gaze. "I need you," my voice croaks.

"Not as much as I need you." His eyes soften, then he slides over me and kisses me. The taste of me on his lips and tongue is strangely familiar, and I like that my scent is all over him.

I kiss him back and then bite his lip. "I need to touch you." I can't keep the frustration out of my voice.

Wes ignores my plea and takes his position once more between my thighs. With added force and speed, his fingers pulse in and out of me. My hips thrust, fucking his hand, but then he lays his other hand on my thigh and, without any effort, holds me still. Wes' tongue licks at my clit while his fingers curl inside of me. Desire builds quickly and the moment he sucks on my clit, I let go. Before I close my eyes, I see Wes lift his head and then I'm showered with color exploding around me.

A few seconds pass and I slowly float back into my body, my breath slowing, and I'm vaguely aware that my hands are free. Wes rolls onto me, his erection pressing into my hip, but I find the energy to push his weight aside so he lands on his back. In one action, I'm straddling him, and my hands grab large palms and hold them near his head. "My turn to take control." I raise my hips to take the solid length of him in, but he grabs me around the waist and stills me above him.

"No. I need to fuck you," he all but growls.

It sounds almost like punishment, but I shake my head. "Let me do this for you."

When his hold loosens, I take the opportunity and slide down on his cock. He exhales loudly and his eyes close momentarily. Lifting my ass slowly, I then sheathe him again and again, quickening the action all while watching his expression glaze over with pleasure. Wes' hands remain tight on my hips. I cover his hands with mine, holding them as though he's controlling me. His eyes round. "Hold on, princess."

His grip tightens, then he lifts me above him and takes over, ramming himself into me. His relentless pounding builds another orgasm. I'm weightless in his grip, like a statue over him, while he fucks me hard. I'm panting, groaning, whispering his name as my body goes limp while being held securely in place. Pleasure builds in that spot deep inside, causing me to lose control and cry out on the edge of climax. Tightening my hand over his, searching for an anchor, I tilt my head back and clench the muscles around his dick, and I come. Wes groans loudly and hisses as he comes, pushing inside me so deep it borders on pain. Then his hands relax and I fall forward to slump over his chest.

I'm listening to his heart while we both glow in aftersex until we drift back into our bodies. I trace the outline of the words across his chest.

With Pain Comes Strength.

"I love you," I whisper. My breath catches at the sincerity in my voice.

The hand tickling my hip stills. He says one word, and it's full of command and promise. "Come." Then he adds in a softer voice, "And be with me."

My lids drift over my eyes to stop the tears. I can't go, and he knows it. But I'm filled with a need to be with him more than to perform. And the pull to be with Wes—and not put my music first—is alien to me. My chest rises and falls quickly. Instead, I say, "How?" because the burn in the back of my throat prevents me from asking more.

"Let me talk to Marshall."

I shake my head. "No. It has to be me. He needs to know how much I want to be with you."

Wes' large hands stroke the length of my back. I curl into him and then I feel him move inside me. Fuck, he's getting hard again.

"I have a plan. But first I have ideas that include you and me." He rolls with me onto my back. "And it's going to take all night to show you just what I have in mind."

I kiss the tip of his nose. "Is that so? Curiosity is my weakness, so how can I object?"

⁓

Waking up to the aroma of coffee in the morning is like being in heaven. Especially after a long night of having enough sex to send me straight to hell. My pussy throbs, prompting the memory. A couple of hours ago we stopped fucking, and I'm not going to cope only on a few hours of sleep.

The gentle kiss on my cheek reminds me that much of last night was also spent making love. I open my eyes to Wes sitting on the bed beside me, coffee in hand. "Thought you might need this."

"You know, it's not going to work out between us with you being a morning person and all." I rub at my eyes and his chuckle sparks a new energy within me. Knowing I can make him laugh, and more importantly make him happy, makes me insanely happy.

"I have to leave this afternoon and don't want to waste any time with you sleeping."

Oh. We hadn't talked about how long he would be here—or why he came in the first place. With my face being the usual traitor to my thoughts, Wes forces a smile as though remembering how the night first began—him finding me with Lena.

"Marshall has his own private plane."

Of course he does.

"When he told me he was coming here overnight, I asked to come with him. Thought I'd surprise you. But he's leaving again at three and I have to return with him."

Neither of us comments on the surprise element.

"Thank you," I whisper and stroke his face. "I'm glad you decided to act impulsively."

"It wasn't impulsive," he says quickly. "I'm always planning on how I can see you, even it's only for a few minutes. When he mentioned it to me, I jumped at the opportunity. You know, I think he can see how miserable I am without you."

I push myself up and sit back against the pillow. Wes ogles my breasts then hands me the coffee. "You think he'll let me come to you?" I ask hopefully.

"No. But I have my ways of getting around him. And if you think about my idea to play in a band—"

I choke on a mouthful of coffee. "Wait. What?"

Wes pats my leg. "I know some guys who are looking for someone to sing and bring fresh ideas to their band. I've always said you have the voice to front one."

"First off, I've never heard you mention this before, so I've never considered it. I'm happy being a DJ." My heart speeds up before the caffeine hits my system. Sudden changes in my life scare the fuck out of me. They remind me of my past and of the dark times when I didn't have choices. But now I do...

"I'm not doing this to scare you. I'm doing it to help you."

I'm blinking at Wes, remembering him saying the same words to me only months before. I trust him now, but I'm still not sure I'm ready for such a big change.

I place my hand over his that's currently resting on the sheet covering my thigh. "How about we first talk to Marshall about me joining a band, then we focus on living together? I'm not an easy person to live with. You might change your mind."

"Yeah. Right." He shakes his head.

"We manage Marshall first."

Wes removes his hand from beneath mine and slowly trails his finger up my arm and over my ink. " Fine." Then he takes the coffee from my hand and pulls the sheet back to reveal the rest of my body. "But first I'm going to make you come, over and over."

2 5

wes

eaving Garnet yesterday was so fucking hard. Not talking to Marshall about her coming to live with me during the flight back to San Fran... even harder. I wanted to fucking punch him for dividing us. But I'm giving her a chance to talk to him, and if Marshall refuses then I'm telling him straight. I could blow up shit on his past, and his sweet little wife wouldn't like some of the truths I have to share.

Pushing thoughts of Marshall from my mind, I order a beer at the bar while I wait for Brand, an old buddy from college, to arrive. We haven't spoken in years, even though we used to be close. In fact, I know very little about what he's been doing with his time after I was drafted and he wasn't. For all I know, he could have stopped playing altogether. I'm interested in hearing what he's done with his life though and where he's now working.

I turn when a strong hand lands on my shoulder. The man standing behind me is smaller than what I remember. Or maybe I just got bigger. Brand's hair is darker and shorter than it was the last time we played together, too. The deep lines around his eyes crinkle when he smiles, and his hand slams into my back, knocking the wind out of me.

"Wes. Good to see you, man." Brand gives me a little shake before we hug with a slap on the back. He ogles my arms, his eyes lowering to my hands. "More ink than I remember, bro."

I shrug. "Is what it is."

"That what you said about the drugs?"

I don't say anything. I nod toward the bar. "You want me to order for you?"

"Sure." He glances at my beer. "Beer's fine."

"So," I say after ordering, "what are you doing with yourself? How did you end up here? I thought you were gonna end up on a ranch and all."

Brand sits on the stool beside me. "Usual story. Met a girl one night in Dallas when I was drowning my sorrows after not getting drafted.

The *drowning* lasted about a year." He laughs sarcastically, and my gut plummets for not checking on him while I celebrated. "But she made everything seem okay. She wasn't from Dallas, so I took a risk and followed her here. Hell, I didn't have anything to lose at that point. The idea of living in 'the Paris of the West' at least gave me something to look forward to... something different." He cocks a shoulder. "Great nightlife, and sports teams," he winks, "and I could watch my buddies play ball. Thought I was set."

I take a swig of my beer. "You never called and said you were at my games. I could have gotten you tickets—"

Brand shakes his head. "I liked watching, but I couldn't talk to you, bro. Hurt too damn much. Had my own way of getting over being a failure, but I could enjoy watching you carve it up."

We drink our beer silently for a while, heads down. Memories are turning like cogs in my head. "Yeah well, I don't really want to talk about the past either. It is what it is," I say again while looking straight ahead and focusing on a bottle of whiskey behind the bar.

"So how did you avoid most of the charges?"

I peer at him sideways. "Marshall." I don't need to say anything more.

His eyes narrow, the brown hue darkening. It reminds me of a determined look he had when we played together. "That bastard still trying to run your life?"

It's my turn to laugh sarcastically. "Yeah, some fathers are like that. Guess I should be grateful. Things could have been a lot worse."

Brand slowly spins his beer in his hand while staring at the bottle as it turns. "He's the reason, ain't he? The reason you didn't care and took the risk, knowing the consequences. Did you do it to piss him off?"

I swipe my hand over my head. "I don't think there was a single reason, man. But if that were the case, well, it backfired. Because now he owns my ass."

"No one owns your ugly ass. Wesley Black Thompson, the quarterback who never gave up, and every fucking one of your teammates played their heart out for you. You were my inspiration, man. What the fuck happened?"

My chest tightens, hearing him talk that way about me. "Lost sight of the reason I played." But that wasn't really it either. My confidence fizzled after my father told me what a loser I was after we lost a game. Told me I was the reason. I could train all I liked and have the body of an athlete, but my brain would always let me down. He always knew how to make me feel worthless. "Not even the sports psychologist could fix me. Guess I wanted out. Out of being under his control... I couldn't see a light at the end of the tunnel." I turn and look at Brand. "You mentioned coming here, said you thought you were set. Are you?"

Brand smiles, showing all of his perfect white teeth. "Married with a kid. Have a stable job as an accountant in Oakland."

"You have a fucking kid? Wait, you got married?" I struggle to hide the shock.

"You were busy." He lowers his head. "I invited some high school friends, no one from college. It was small, and most of the guests were from Jenny's side."

I place an arm on his shoulder. "Congrats, man. Jenny's a lucky woman."

"Yeah, I'll have to introduce you so you can tell her that." We both laugh.

"And a kid." I shake my head then take another chug. "Girl or boy?"

"A boy. His name is Wesley, after you."

I choke. "You fucking serious?"

Brand nods. "He's six, and loves the game. Told him he could meet you someday. He wants to play peewee football, but I think he's too young. Besides, I don't want to coach. Know of anyone?" He gives me a sidelong glance.

"You can't be fucking serious? Me?"

"You're perfect. You know the dangers, and unlike other dads who want their sons to grow up to be the best damn player in the whole of fucking America, you know the importance of hitting and getting hit safely, and enjoying the game for what it is. Figured it would be good for you. Hey, they don't even keep score."

I've experienced first-hand the type of father he's referring to. My gut tightens at the prospect of doing something for the game I once loved... and for the kids. Plus I owe Brand, because I feel as though I'd let him down. "Will your league allow a player suspended on drug charges to coach? I highly doubt it."

"What were your charges? Did they stand or did Marshall get you off?"

He has a point. Marshall got the charges dropped by a technicality, but I was still banned from playing for other reasons. Didn't stop the media from having a field day and making me look like a fucking drug addict before it went to court.

And speaking of the media... coaching would make it look even more like I'm getting my life back on track. Wouldn't hurt with Marshall either and could be a start to not being the loser he thinks I am.

"If you're serious about me coaching, then I'll get things moving and talk to Marshall."

Brand places his hand on my shoulder and squeezes it. "You're a good man, Wes.

garnet

My hands tremble as I wait outside Marshall's office.

The blond receptionist has the perfect look of a make-up model and the body of a Victoria Secret supermodel. In her tight navy pencil skirt and white low-cut blouse, she glides across the floor effortlessly, her head held high and shoulders back, with the confidence I need before I enter Marshall's private meeting room.

When Marshall called earlier today and asked to meet with me, I'd assumed Wes had mentioned something to him. I sent Wes a text asking if he'd spoken to Marshall about us, but his response didn't indicate that at all.

No. I promised I'd wait for you to talk to him. Have you changed your mind? Do you want me to talk to him?

So why does Marshall want to see me?

Before I have time to ponder further, the blond receptionist calls my name and I follow her through heavy, double wooden doors.

"Afternoon, Mister Thompson. Miss Delaware is here." She steps aside and allows me to pass, then closes the door behind her.

Marshall stands from his desk and walks around to greet me. "Would you care for a drink?"

"No, thank you." As soon as Marshall turns his back, my gaze darts around the room, taking in the cedar furnishings and white walls with massive paintings. Fuck, the framed art alone probably costs more than my apartment. I'm stunned, staring out of the floor-to-ceiling windows that overlook downtown LA.

Marshall pours red wine from a decanter. "How are you enjoying working at Red Star?"

I spin around. "It's as good as I imagined."

Marshall sips his red wine then peers at me over the rim of the glass. "I've heard you want to be the main act, not just on Sunday nights."

Heat creeps up into my cheeks and I nod. I'm annoyed that I allow this man to get to me, that I feel insignificant when I'm around him. "Yes, I would, but—"

"Then allow me to tell you how happy I am with your performance, and that Thursday and Friday nights are also yours."

Part of me wants to punch the air and jump with excitement, the other part slumps. How do I say I'm hoping to move to San Fran when he's just promoted me? "That's awesome. Thank you."

He nods and grins like he's done me a huge favor. "I take it you enjoyed your time with my son over the weekend?"

"Um, yes. It was great to see him. He told me how much he's enjoying San Fran and his new job."

Marshall sips more wine before answering. "The kid's surprised me. He's excelling there. Looks like it's worked out fine for both of you. I know you have this fling going on, but if you know what's right for you, then you'll end it before it ruins both of your careers."

I flinch at his tone. My mouth opens, realizing that he believes I'm the bad blood in the relationship. I struggle to find the words to respond, knowing he thinks I'm no good for Wes.

"I'll have Julia email you the details." He checks his wristwatch. "If you'll excuse me, I have a board meeting to attend. They'll be glad to hear that bar sales and the number of customers have increased since you've joined us." He walks to the door and holds it open for me. "I'll have to stick around one night and watch you perform."

His tone is flat like he's bored and holds no promise. All I manage is a nod before I scamper out of his office and toward the elevator. When I reach the ground floor, I pull out my cell and call Wes to try and explain what the hell just happened because my head is still whirling.

"What do you mean you've accepted another contract?" Wes presses—loudly.

I jerk the phone from my ear. "I don't know how it happened..." I step out onto the street and squint when the sun beats down on my face.

"Why didn't you tell me? And why the hell didn't you take Xavier with you?"

"I thought I could manage him," I whisper.

"Xavier and I are here to help you. Let us do the negotiating. Never mind, I'll talk to him. I miss you like fucking hell, so I'm taking the weekend off and coming to see you."

I close my eyes and let out a long breath. I want to say, "Don't, I'll be fine," but I'd be lying. "See you Friday then."

The average age in The Rox tonight would have to be around twenty-one. Maybe I wore blinders when I performed here, but I can't remember the crowd being so young. Could be that Claire is younger than me and she appeals to a younger crowd. Fuck knows how half of the chicks got past security because they don't look much older than seniors in high school.

More puzzling is how I ended up here on a Tuesday night. The kiss I shared with Lena wasn't the reason, but it reminded me how I miss her friendship... miss *our* friends.

Even the bartender is new. I order a whiskey then saunter to a corner where I can check out the crowd. My gaze shoots to the stage when Claire hollers to the crowd. Everyone roars in appreciation when she plays her first track. Not a bad beat, though not one I'd use. The teen chicks seem to like it and start bouncing around the dance floor. They either haven't danced in a club before or are blind drunk. Could be both.

I down the remainder of my drink and keep the glass in hand as I meander through the crowd to the corner where my gals usually hang out. I freeze when I see Lena on Peta's lap. Their lips are locked and Lena's hips grind on Peta. Even from here, I can see Peta's hand between Lena's thighs, working her. I hiss out a breath and look away to Sheila, Kate and Becky, sitting opposite. Once I'm over the initial shock of seeing Lena making out, I head over to the group, jingling the ice in my glass as though it were a compass leading the way.

Kate is the first to spot me and she springs from her seat, bounding toward me. "Hey, girl. It's good to see you."

"And you," I say, smiling as she hugs me. "Haven't seen you at Red Star, so I thought I should pay you all a visit."

Kate takes my hand and leads me to a spare chair. "Look who I found, y'all."

Becky and Sheila scream and both embrace me with the welcoming I'd hoped for. Peta and Lena are slower. Peta hugs me, but all I get from Lena is a nod. I look to the stage where Claire is hitting the decks. "She's doing alright."

"She's ripping it up." Lena gives me a challenging look.

"I'm happy for her," I say honestly, not taking Lena's bait. She turns back to Peta, curling into her side.

"Tell us all about Red Star," Sheila yells when the music cranks up a notch. "And that hot guy of yours."

I smile at Sheila, my heart swelling at the mention of Wes. "Not a lot to tell." I wink at her.

Sheila punches my arm. "Come and sit, because you're not leaving until we hear all the gossip on you two."

I glance over to Lena. She's back to sitting on Peta's lap. She appears happy.

And I'm happy.

So if I can handle her face-fucking Peta, then she can surely handle me being back in the group.

wes

fter the almost silent plane trip to LA, I leave Marshall and head to Red Star where Gar is performing tonight.

The line to get into the club is around the corner. Striding past the queue, I merely nod at security and I'm allowed to enter. Making my way to the bar, I mentally assess the crowd and compare it to my new venue. Yeah, the club is bigger in San Fran, but I think Gar is pulling in higher numbers.

After chugging my first beer, I take the second and find a dark corner near the stage so I can watch Gar inconspicuously. Neon lights flash on. Bright lights dart across the dance floor. Like a spark of electricity, synthesized sounds fill the room and girls flock to the dance floor—

not to dance but to get as close to Gar as possible.

Gar walks out onto the stage. She waves one hand, and stares into the bright lights. The crowd responds by screaming and jumping before she plays a single note.

"Hello," she calls out, smiling her winning smile. As soon as the first note plays out, her fans squeal, and I smile and cringe at the same time. The tempo escalates, then she raises her hand in the air and yells, "Show me your hands people so I know you're fucking alive."

For a moment, I yank my gaze away from the hot DJ and scan the crowd, absorbing the way they respond to her energy, the adoration showing in their expressions. Then I catch how the guys are drooling and I'm nauseous with irritation.

The sound of Gar's voice pulls my attention back to the stage. She's singing a melody, cranking the deck so it mixes with synthesized music and a rapper mix. It's fucking brilliant. The lyrics are unfamiliar, which is odd because I've heard all of Gar's tracks. That can only mean that she's been busy creating new tracks while I've been away.

Gar's words filter through the room like the sound of a harp. The impact of her voice combined with an unconventional rhythm draws every person's soul to hers, touching them in a way so they reach out to her.

At the end of the song, she holds one hand in the air. The crowd applauds but she skips straight into the next song, her eyes never leaving the deck. Her raised hand pumps the air, then she smiles to the crowd. It's a favorite of hers, a trendy beat, and I like what she's done with it. Gar starts bouncing when the rhythm switches, and the lights flash across the masses in tune to her vibes. Even if her fans wanted to dance to her raves, it's standing room only on the bottom level.

Meandering back through the crowd to the bar, objections hit me like wrecking balls why I shouldn't take her away from all of this. It's her dream, and as much as I believe she'll make it in a band, her first and only love is being a DJ. I can't do it to her. And Marshall won't transfer her to San Fran while fans are flocking to her here.

LA is *her* home.

So the only alternative—for now—is to do the long-distance thing and be miserable while we're apart. My gut tightens, the truth hitting hard.

"What can I get you?" the bartender asks quickly.

I hesitate, deciding I need something stronger than a beer. "Give me four zombie shots."

The bartender nods. "You want a tray to carry them back to your table?"

"Nope. I'll drink them here at the bar."

After downing each shot, I catch a cab back to my house and immediately strip my clothes off, hoping a midnight swim will help clear my mind. And while the shock of the cold water certainly has a way of bringing my thoughts into focus, it also leaves me physically spent but wide awake.

Lying in my bed, all I can think about is Gar and how much I need her beside me. My cock throbs as I recall the last time we were together, how willingly she opened her sweet thighs for me. I stroke my dick and it feels so fucking good. Images of the two of us storm my mind... on my kitchen counter, in the shower, on the balcony. My eyes remain closed as I pump my hand harder, my head filled with delicious images of Garnet.

Just as I'm imagining the taste of her on my tongue, the mattress dips and my eyes fling open. There's only one other person with a key to my home...

The dim moonlight filters in between the crack of the curtains, creating the perfect silhouette around her body. Gar stares at me, then her gaze lowers to my hand still wrapped around my cock.

"Didn't want to wait for me?" I can't see her expression in the dark, yet the double entendre is clear as day. The last thing I want to do is hurt her, and the tone of her voice tells me she's hurting. I reach up and take her cheeks between my hands, kissing her gently. Slowly, I guide her until she's lying on top of me. The warmth of her lips fills the void in my heart, so I kiss her like there's no tomorrow... and frankly, I don't know how much time we have left. I want her—and all she has to offer—but I'm not thinking about me. Instead, I'm doing what's best for Gar because she means everything to me, and I can't take her dream away.

Finding the straps of her shirt, I slide them down her shoulders, concentrating on keeping in control and not giving in to my desire to rip her clothes from her body. After more kisses, I dispose of her top and bra. She stands and I watch silently as she shimmies out of her jeans and panties.

Lifting the sheet, I offer her my bed. It's more than a request or invitation. It's the sacred spot beside me in between the sheets, where only a soulmate deserves to be. This isn't sex or a quick fuck. This is an offer of my heart. And if she takes it—no matter what happens after tonight—it will belong to her.

Gar slides in beside me, and the heat of her body next to mine flicks a switch. Without wasting another second, I'm on top of her, covering her in kisses. My hips fall between her open thighs. "You'll always be mine," I say with more aggression than I intend.

Gar's hand slips behind my neck, and just before I drive my dick inside of her, she whispers, "I always have been."

garnet

ou need to be street smart. Think safe," Xavier says before I walk out the back door of Red Star.

I give a short cynical laugh. The dark streets used to be my home. There's seriousness behind his eyes. So I nod. Once.

"Always am."

"Have you received further hate on social media? Any mention of Lena?"

I shake my head. A lie. Her trolls are still at it. Telling me I'm a bitch, and fucked in the head and how could I do this to her.

"No threats?"

"No," I say firmly, and yank the hood of my white sweater over my head. "I need to think. Walking clears my mind. Then I'll grab a cab home."

"Home?" Xavier frowns.

Wes' Malibu house is my home for now until I work out where I want to live.

"See you in a couple of days." I push open the side door of Red Star and allow the cool night air to hit my face. I inhale, deep. Catch a whiff of stale urine, and the standard scent of cum lingering in the alley.

I look right and left before stepping out further into the darkness. There's a couple of silhouettes staggering, the last to be booted from the club at two in the morning.

Wrapping my arms around my middle, I hear the door close behind me. Aware Xavier's watching a few seconds longer before locking it.

Xavier's uncomfortable with me wanting to walk alone. But it's my routine since Wes left two weeks ago. We've barely talked. I get that he's giving me space so I can think about his proposition.

The thought of not being up on the stage and doing what I love is eating me up. Until tonight, being hit with a reversal of emotion, I struggled to get excited about my performance when I thought about what happens next if I decline. The empty feeling in my gut of continuing on without Wes in my life left me flat before I went out on stage.

Xavier noticed, assumed it was the hate on social media.

Hate, I can deal with.

I reach Third Street Promenade, and instead of looking out for a cab I keep walking.

Pulling out my cell, I stare at the blank screen a few more seconds before stuffing it back into my pocket.

I should call him.

Tell him tonight was like a hit of cocaine, and I'm on my way home.

...

...

He would see through the lie.

...

...

What is he doing right now?

Has Marshall got in his ear?

Fuck!

I keep walking until I reach the pier.

There are more people around than usual this time of night. I get a hit of a familiar aroma as I pass a group of boys with a lit joint which is be-ing passed between them. I find a free area on the rail, lean over and peer down to the dark water circling the worn support posts below. Lights reflect over the surface in a multitude of reflective color. The shapes almost geometric and reminding me of my erratic thoughts blending from one crazy one to the next.

There are circles of life, I fucking get that. Do I want to uproot everything I have here? If Wes could come back to LA and...

Fuck you, Marshall.

I push off the rail with force and turn only to bump into a guy. He grunts.

"My bad." I hold up both arms.

His brow pulls to a V studying my face. He doesn't respond.

The hood of my sweater conceals my hair.

My face exposed.

Sidestepping around him I head toward the street. Two yellow cabs are in the distance.

Boots pound the ground behind me. The step quickening. I don't turn, only interpret the closeness and listen for voices in conversation. I reach the cab and with my hand on the door glance over my shoulder.

A guy stops while others walk around him. He stares, shoves his hands in his pocket and continues slowly toward me. *Was it the guy I bumped into?*

Letting it go, I climb in and give directions to Wes' Malibu address.

Leaning back in the seat, I close my eyes and inhale a long breath.

My heart refuses to slow.

The last time I glanced at the clock, it was almost four.

Pushing the sheet aside I jump out of bed and pace.

Coffee or booze won't help. I consider drugs, the pharmaceutical kind, but a voice rears up warning me of another ugly road if I choose to take it.

Yanking the thick curtains apart I look out to the ocean. There's an eerie silence with only the waves breaking the shoreline and not far from the house. I open the doors, a slight breeze blows through the curtain but not cold enough for me to cover my naked body. Stepping out to the balcony I make out the ocean several strides from the base of the steps. The beach is deserted so I bound down the steps, feel the squish of sand between my toes, then the wetness around my ankles. A few more steps and I dive.

It's like being blindfolded.

A risk that comforts my soul.

The cold water is a refreshing shock, and when I surface a shiver rips through my body. I flop back to float over a wave and stare momentarily toward the stars, twinkling in a cloudless night sky. I differentiate the planets from the stars with a crescent moon not giving much light.

Flipping up to my feet I wade through the surf to the sand. Dusting my feet as I walk the wooden stairs to the balcony. Using the shower hose located at the top gate, I wash the remaining sand from my soles and a quick rinse over my entire body, including between my legs. Sandy vaginas are not my thing. I flop onto the sun lounge and tilt my head back. It's liberating to lie here in the dark, naked, on millionaire row, and bake under a moon that sees your soul.

The universe, the stars and planets ground my thoughts when I think about my purpose. When the sun is beating down everyone scurries about believing their daily lives are fulfilled, and their individual existence is complete.

Under the stars, the darkness finds truth and meaning. Our planet is a small fragment in the universe, and yet we take all it offers for granted. Ironic that my best work is at night only under artificial lighting, waiting for creatures of the night to come out to play. It's a time that can bring out the worst, allow the inner demons free reign.

In this moment, staring up to the heavens, I'm mesmerized, and filled with gratitude.

2 9

garnet

A creak.

Seagulls squawk.

My eyes shutter open, adjust.

The sun will soon rise. Curtains wave in the breeze to my left.

Shit! I left the doors wide open.

"Morning, Garnet."

I feel the sharp point on my neck before I can turn my head in the direction of the voice.

"No quick movements. I don't want to slip," he slurs.

My thoughts catch up. Run through the process of what to do if threatened. The same process I used when on the streets.

Only I can't see the person with a knife to my neck. A guy, going by the deep tone of his voice. A knife I assume by the sharp point.

What if it's glass? A broken bottle?

My heart pounds hard against my ribs. "What do you want?"

He chuckles.

"From me," I add.

"Now we're talking."

I need him to keep talking to lower his guard even though I'm in a vulnerable position on my back. Naked. He's out of my line of sight, and my reach. My breath quickens.

"How long have you been here?"

"Watching you long enough to have a boner that's twitching for action." He chuckles again. "Heard stories about your rose. Looks damn pretty in the flesh. And those nipple rings. Who gets you off? Lena and her petite lips or that cocky baller you're fucking? Suppose this is all his?"

The knife presses a little harder into my neck.

"Who would you bleed for? Him or her?"

"What do you want from me?" I repeat.

Voices carry in the wind. But they're too far in the distance.

"Don't try anything stupid," he growls.

I close my eyes and will my fight or flight response to slow so I can calm my racing heart.

Hell, I'm breathing so damn fast I'm close to hyperventilating. I need to gather my thoughts.

Do what he asks and wait for the right time to react or run.

"Stand up."

I push forward—the sharp to my neck is gone. Then it's on my lower back. I consider what organ he could damage, and realize it's a better option than my jugular. I stand and face the ocean, consider running until I feel piercing pressure on my back.

"Go inside, bitch."

I turn as I pass the glass doors and catch part of his reflection. Jeans and a sweater I recognize from hours earlier. "You followed me?"

"Wasn't hard. Followed you in a cab. Access to this beach is only a mile down the road. Walked until I saw you lying here, legs spread waiting for my cock. You made it *easy* for me to find you. *Easy.*"

We enter Wes' bedroom. "Why?"

I move slightly toward the mirror in the corner. Stare at our dark reflections. Take him in. Assess the distance between us. He realizes, and our gaze meets in the glass. He moves quickly to my side. His body pinning my left arm. His erection pushing into my hip. His left arm around my chest, his hand pinning my right arm. The knife now coming from behind in his right hand. The blade resuming its post on my neck. The knife is larger than I anticipated, longer than a flick knife and capable of more damage.

"Skinny bitch aren't you." His slimy tongue touches my cheek then he licks the side of my face.

I block out the vulgarity. Note the weed on his breath. It's a moment in time where he's distracted by his sexual thoughts. An opening to react as he might still be high.

I don't think only move by instinct.

In a forceful action, I push my elbows out to create a gap between us and drop to my knees. He watches it play out in the glass before he turns his attention back, so I'm one step ahead. The blade had slid up toward my ear but I'm free. My elbow slams into his balls and erection. He cupules over and I shoot another blow to his throat aiming for the Adam's apple. I spring up and chop the arm holding the knife.

He groans, stumbles, and drops the knife all in a mere second. Scooping the knife from the floor, I spin and step back welding it in his direction. He remains slumped gasping for breath. A hand bracing his groin, the other on his throat.

Hell, he's an amateur.

Nevertheless, my heart still pounds hard.

"What the fuck are you doing here?" I yell at him. "Why did you follow me?"

"You broke my dick," he squeaks.

"I'm going to break more than your fucking dick!" I scream back.

He springs up, and I prepare to lunge at him, but he's out the bedroom door and hobbling down the balcony steps before I can take my next breath. Slamming the doors shut I lock both doors, stand back and stare out the glass to watch him stumbling as he attempts to run in the sand.

Call the police.

Call Wes.

Breathe.

Breathe.

My knees give way and I collapse to the floor. A drop of blood lands near my fingers. I become aware of the sting to the side of my face. I'm too scared to look but I need to evaluate the damage. The physical damage at least. Finding a small amount of energy I push up and stumble to the bathroom. Blood treacle lines my face. Splashing water over the area I'm filled with relief. The first cut is over the bony prominence of my jaw, the other near my ear. Both an inch in length.

Not deep.

I inhale and think how it could have ended. Was he just a punk who was bored and thought he'd follow me for kicks because he was high? Or was it more? I should call the police…

It would gather more negative attention. The trolls will turn it around and say I'm playing the victim. I know how they roll.

Under the spray of the shower I consider options.

I'm not staying here another night in case the bastard decides to come back.

Xavier will be all *I told you so*.

Wes will…

… make me leave.

30

wes

"What a week." Fleur has an exasperated expression as we walk out of the office block.

"Yeah," I concede. "I'm wrecked and want to collapse and sleep a week but a new band's playing tonight and I'm going to watch them rehearse."

"Lotus?"

"Yeah."

"I heard them jam. They're sick." Fleur smiles. "I might also head there if you don't mind me trailing along?"

I consider going home to an empty apartment.

"Come on." Fleur links her arm in mine. "Let's grab a drink first. Recharge a little. You should try and relax." Her brown eyes twinkle beneath long lashes.

She tugs on my arm and I just go with her, since the closest bar to our office is one hundred yards away. Our arms remain linked before we sit on a barstool. "A beer, big fella?"

I pat my guts. "Ease up. I've been working out."

Fleur's eyes hood. "I've heard the rumors," she purrs. "Quite a reputation."

"Don't believe all you hear," I say, less than impressed.

The barman places two frothy beers before us.

"Cheers to the weekend." She clinks my glass. "Any plans?"

I take a swig and enjoy the sensation of the cold liquid coating my throat. "Nope, you?" I should have plans. If not visit, at least call or message Gar. Hell, we haven't spoken in two weeks. It's not a standoff, more an understanding of giving the other space. Time to think. She knows how I feel about her. Told her she will always be mine. Every nerve warns me she can't come here. She needs to do what she loves, follow her dream. She loves me. Still my gut tells me it's not enough. She can survive without love. She's done it before.

The question is can I survive without her?

"Ease up there." Fleur hails the barman. "Better give him another."

I stare into an empty glass. "Thanks."

Fleur's hand squeezes my thigh. "Don't want you going home early before Lotus takes the stage." Her hand settles high, too close to my groin for a friendly gesture.

I feel nothing.

Even worse I do nothing about it. I should remove her hand but I don't. And I don't encourage her either.

"I'm going to finish this beer and drive to the club. So you think Lotus will crush it?"

She smiles. "Hell, yes. Hundred bucks they'll be your main act in a few months."

That gets a brow raise. "That confident?"

"When it comes to impressing you, yes." Her hand rubs a circle over my pants. "You haven't been yourself lately. You mope at the office."

"I don't mope. I'm distracted. Got a bit going on, and when I'm like that I detach myself from everyone around me."

"Marshall's a ball breaker we all know it. But you need a balance. Lately, you're all work-

work. Heard you even went for a quick trip with him down to LA."

I hold her gaze. "That was to see my girl-friend."

Red lips part. Her brow pinches. "The gay DJ?"

"Yeah. She's bi. And now she's with me." I chug the remains of my beer.

"Right." Her hand slides away. "I didn't think you two were an item. I thought she was like a toy to you."

I choke on the last mouthful. "I don't treat girls like toys..." she shoots me a look, "... any-more."

She nods. "Well, Wesley Black, if you ever want to chat..." she raises her glass as though it's the alcohol talking, "... and fuck, you know where to find me."

I nod. "Chat, yeah. My father has a rule about fucking work colleagues."

"Isn't Garnet a work colleague?"

I swivel the glass in one hand, loosen the top buttons of my shirt with the other. "Yeah."

"So break another rule if you need to de-stress. I'm attracted to you. Find you hot-as-fuck."

The words don't sound right coming from her sweet lips.

"Unless you don't find me attractive..."

My gaze roams down involuntarily, over her pert breasts. The top button of her blouse is undone, and only now I notice her cleavage. She swivels in the chair so her legs open a little toward me. "Restroom sex can be so much fun."

I let out a long breath. Not so long ago I would have taken her up on the offer. Fucked her sexy ass over a basin and not care who saw.

"It's not attraction because you're one sexy lady. I'm not the right guy for you." I throw some bills on the bar and stand.

Fleur downs her beer and stands ready to follow me.

"I'll walk back to the car park with you. I hate walking to my car alone in underground parking lots."

I nod. I'm not a bastard. "Let's go then."

garnet

An hour ago on the street opposite his office, I watched a brunette link arms with Wes and head toward a bar.

Rattled from what happened last night I wasn't thinking clearly. The bewilderment started when I was too scared to shut my eyes and jumped up, headed to the airport to catch the next flight to San Fran. I knew Xavier would take care of my gig in LA since he's been telling me for weeks to take a break.

I didn't think, only acted, by running to the one person who could make me feel—or not feel anything but his body wrapped around me because *only I* can make myself feel safe. The more I thought about the fucker breaking in and almost assaulting me, the more I blame myself for acting recklessly. I doubt it was premeditated, more he recognized me walking the street alone, and decided to do something dumb. And I've met my fair share of dumb fuckers over the years. Yet, it shook me enough that I couldn't remain in the house alone. I wanted to be with the one guy who cares about me the most.

So I thought...

From a safe distance through the glass I observed them, watched her hand on his thigh, the batter of lashes—every flirtatious move—while he did nothing. Then I fled not being able to watch anymore.

The old me would have stormed in, yelled obscenities at him, knocked her pretty ass of the stool.

Too much hurt has passed my thin armor, dimming the fire in my soul.

I raise my cell and look at the blank screen.

Is she the reason for his silence?

Not that I blame him, she's gorgeous. I'd fuck her too if my heart didn't belong to him.

I think of everything he had said to me. The memory like a knife to my heart, my conscience screaming to trust no one. The cut to my face throbs like a bitch. Early stages of healing I tell myself, and a reminder to harden the fuck up.

The thought fails to stop tears welling from pain, and the invisible knife in my chest, as my heart splits into two.

I pull up maps to find the nearest hotel.

"Gar?"

I swivel.

"Hell, what happened to you?" Peta rushes over and pulls me to her chest. After all that's happened she's still a friend.

"A long story." I choke back tears. "Hey." I smile. "What are you doing here?"

"Lena and I thought we'd head here for the weekend. Check out the famous San-Fran Red Star. Are you playing?"

Lena's here.

"Sadly no gig here. Came to surprise Wes. I needed a break. Spoke to Xavier, and of course, he made it happen."

"And your face... what did you do?"

I lift a finger and skate it over the white dressing. "Tripped and fell on the corner of the coffee table. Could've been worse."

She nods, her eyes assessing me. "We're having drinks in the hotel bar." She nods to the building a few doors up. "Want to join us?"

More than anything.

3 2

garnet

ena stands from the bar stool when she notices I'm with Peta.

"Look who I found wandering the street." Peta leaves my side and whispers in her ear. I assume she's asking permission to bring me along like I'm a pet dog or something.

"A coincidence I promise." I nod at Lena. "I'm cool if three's a crowd."

"No, no. Of course, it's fine." She plants a kiss on Peta's cheek, lowers her rear and turns to the bar. My shout. What can I get you?"

I edge closer, lean on the bar. Hell, in a few seconds I acknowledge how good she looks. Her hair is longer, straighter, and she appears toned. *Fit.* Her face is a work of art, as though the makeup was professionally applied. I glance to

Peta and realize hers matches, yet I didn't notice earlier as she lacks the high cheekbones, and fuck-me eyes that set Lena apart from other girls.

"You both look good," I say honestly.

"Thanks to you." Lena grins. She tilts her head studying my expression. "You didn't like this dress, remember?"

"Right." I have no idea what clothing Lena took from the gifts sent to me by the top fashion designers. It should anger me but it doesn't. "You know we should get a photo so I can tag the designer."

My new code is *deconflict*.

She glances at Peta, a look for silent approval before giving a nod.

I hand my cell to the barman who takes a quick snap. Perusing over the images I note full body length.

Tick.

Arms around each other's shoulders.

Tick.

As it will work for us both. For Lena and Peta to get in good with the designers and for me, so the trolls will hopefully let it be.

"So who are the labels?"

Names roll off her tongue without a glance at tags.

I hand my cell to Peta. You're an Insta wiz with all the hashtags. She smiles as though I've handed her a brick of gold.

And I smile in thanks for the distraction.

In the few seconds I wait for Peta to finish tapping, I sense Lena staring. "What happened to your face?"

I open my mouth but Peta interrupts, "She fell and landed on a coffee table. Could've been worse."

I nod. Then answer her silent question, "Peta asked when she saw me out front."

Peta passes me my cell. "What do you think?"

I'm impressed she asked me to check. It looks fine, so I post it and push my cell in my pocket then step back when Lena takes a step closer to inspect my face. Fingers grip my chin as she turns my face, angling my cheek to the light. "There's no discharge. I can fix it so no one will notice.

"I thought the pharmacist did a good job. And when did you become a makeup artist?" I laugh.

"I started the course when we were together. You were too busy to notice." There's no bitterness to her tone, only that she's stating a fact. She passes me a wine glass, and another to Peta.

"Wine? No shots?"

She gives me a look. "I like wine. Even more the crystal I drink it out of."

Sounds about right. I chug half the glass in one effort. Glance up to Lena studying me over the rim of her glass.

Being here, talking to her like this is unnerving me more than I want to admit. Yet, I'm not sure where to go because Wes has fucked up my plans.

"Let me fix your dressing," Lena says innocently. "I might surprise you?"

"You did that on a regular basis." I take another swig of white wine and decide I do like the taste. Both Peta and Lena are staring at me. I grin, and they laugh, finally comprehending I'm playing with them.

"So, do you want to come upstairs?"

wes

otus finish their first song and the small gathering applauds. I give the thumbs up and look to the sound tech who does the same.

"We're set." I smile at Fleur.

She's clapping enthusiastically and beaming her smile at the lead singer.

My cell buzzes in my suit jacket. I raise a finger and leave the room when I notice its Marshall.

"Where are you?"

"At Red Star watching Lotus perform in prep for tonight's gig. Why the fuck do you care?"

"Here?"

"Yes, here."

"You didn't tell me Garnet needed time off to do whatever she needs to do. I thought you must have put her up to it and arranged a secret rendezvous.”

“What?”

“You heard.”

“Gar’s having time off? To do what?”

“I thought you would know the answer. I’m getting back to her manager. He might know more by now.”

“By now? What the fuck does that mean? He didn’t before?”

“He rang the club and said she needed the time off to recharge. That’s it.”

“When?” I stare at the blank screen and curse.

I call Gar.

Voicemail.

“Hey, babe. What are you doing this weekend? I’m at the club watching this new band perform. Lotus. Ever heard of them?”

I hang up. So fucking lame. We haven’t spoken in two weeks, and that’s what I say. I’m a douchebag. A worried douchebag.

I pull up Xavier’s number. Voice mail again.

Fuck.

The door opens and Lotus’ manager pokes his head inside. “They’re ready to play. You coming back in?”

I nod.

I watch the young guys with long locks play their hearts out. Only I don't hear a word of it. I'm too caught up thinking why my girlfriend would take a weekend off and not tell me.

I send a text to Xavier.

What's up with Gar pulling out of her gig tonight?

Seconds later he replies.

Thought you'd know that answer. She's not responding to my calls or texts.

I stand and wave to the technician.

"Sounds sick guys. I'm heading out for a bite. See you back here in a couple of hours."

I'm not out the door when I try her number again.

Voicemail.

Son of a bitch.

"Gar, call me. Now."

garnet

t's oddly relaxing to sit with my head tilted back. My eyes shut while Lena applies makeup, dabbing it over the new skin-colored dressing she reapplied.

"How's that?" she asks Peta.

I lift my head.

Peta nods approvingly.

Lena straddles me. Neither her nor Peta seem to care about the way she tilts her pelvis at my hands in my lap. Through hooded eyes I watch her inner thigh skim my fingers as she slides slowly, gently, the action as thoughtful as the brushstrokes on my face.

I know she's teasing me. I can see through her deadpan expression.

Peta's on her third glass of white wine in the short time I've been here. "Ready for a refill?" Peta asks.

I nod. Desperate for more alcohol.

"Keep your head still," Lena instructs. "And I'll have a glass of champagne, babe."

She sits.

On my hands.

Our gazes lock. Something passes between us, a combination of attraction, jealousy, and revenge.

I want to curl my fingers but I don't. Only I flatten my fingers so there's no ridge to grind her clit over.

Fuck she's wet.

Her body weight sinks harder and I stop myself from groaning. "Surprised?"

That's she's wet for me?

"Lena has always had a flair for art," Peta says from the kitchen. "You shouldn't be surprised how good she is at this."

She grins knowing Peta has no clue.

"Wes is going to want to fuck you the moment he sees you. I'm that good," she sings. "Which reminds me. Peta can you grab bunny ears and put her on charge."

"I'm sure Gar doesn't want to hear you talk about bunny."

Her gaze bores into mine. "Gar doesn't care that we had one hell of a session before going down to the bar. My pussy is so damn sore. Sorry if you can smell me. I get wet easily thinking about how Peta makes me orgasm. Bunny is more for her. Peta has the best fingers after years playing the piano."

Peta doesn't hear any of it, as she's in the bedroom fetching I assume 'bunny.'

"Your pussy doesn't seem sore now," I whisper.

She smiles and grinds a little harder. "Close your eyes, Gar. I have your left eye to finish."

I should push her off.

I should go to Wes but who is he with? My heart races thinking about it. I flinch when she pats near my cuts. Swallow down the burn. Being here, Lena doing this is taking my mind off why I came to San Fran.

When she finishes my face, all three of us intend to head to Red Star.

They believe I'm surprising Wes. The surprise is on me. Especially now with Lena egging me on as though she wants my fingers to accidentally slip.

"I'm ready for that wine," I call out to Peta. "Lena's taking longer here than I expected." After a few wines it no longer feels unnatural to have Lena on my lap, grinding innocently.

"Just like old times, babe," she whispers.

I glare at her. Is she saying I had trouble making her orgasm? I turn my fingers and push up. Hard. She gasps and lifts her ass a little.

"Sorry, my cell's buzzing in my pocket. I need to get it."

She snatches it from my hand and reads the screen. "It's Wes and Xave. Both want you to call them. They can wait. I'm almost done."

She glances over her shoulder, and checks Peta's out of sight, then leans close to my ear. "Put your fingers back on your lap."

She leans back, our eyes lock with understanding.

I have no idea what game she's playing but I'm not about to damage the small steps of rebuilding a friendship with Peta. Though leaving and being alone to my thoughts isn't an option right now.

Peta walks back into the room and I keep my hands at my side, closing my eyes to block out Lena's glare.

wes

otus play into their fourth track when my cell buzzes in my pocket. I yank it out hoping its Gar.

Xavier.

She's fine. Needed a break and told me not to worry. Neither should you.

"*I* shouldn't worry?" I murmur sarcastically to myself. I shake my head.

I'm staring at a blank screen wishing her name would light it up.

Where are you?

To hell with Xavier telling me what to do. If she doesn't answer by the end of the night I'm catching the first red-eye flight tomorrow.

The hours pass slowly. My enthusiasm for Lotus now a fraction of the admiration echoing from the crowd. I down another beer, keeping a low profile near the front corner of the club. It's almost eleven and the main band will be taking the stage soon. I don't need to stay. Someone else is demanding my attention.

Before I leave, Fleur comes to my side. "What do you think?"

"Going by the crowd's response my opinion is irrelevant."

Her mouth opens in surprise.

I smile and give her a thumbs up. "Consider Lotus signed, little fangirl."

"I need to be honest with you." She screws up her face a little. "My brother is the drummer. I didn't want your decision to be a conflict of interest."

I turn back to the stage. Take further notice of the guy with the dark dreads. Wouldn't have picked it with her schoolgirl appearance. "He's quite the performer."

Her smile almost reaches ear to ear.

"Anyway, I'm outta here. See you Monday."

Making my way through the crowd I type out another message to Gar.

Heading home now. Call me please. Otherwise, I'm catching the next red-eye to LA.

I'm almost at the back of the club when a pretty blonde steps into my path.

"I'm not in LA," she screams over the music.

It takes me a moment for my brain to catch up to my stunned expression. My gaze roams over her in a short dress that barely covers her assets, her blonde cropped hair curled to flatter her face, and thick make up that doesn't look wrong on her. Every glance seduces me little by little. My dick twitches until I remember why I'm pissed and worried about her equally. I want to grab her, pull her into my arms until Lena places an arm around Gar's shoulder like it's the most natural thing to do.

"She looks hot, doesn't she? You can thank me later."

My gaze remains on Gar, stuck on those fuck-me eyes. "What's going on? I mean... wow, you're here!"

"Surprise." Gar smiles. It's a pathetic effort and it screams something's up.

"I was about to head home." I glance at Peta who's looking a little uncomfortable, and then Lena. "Sorry to be rude, it's been one helluva week." Gar avoids my gaze so I lean closer. "How are you here?"

"Flights frequently run from LA to San Fran."

I narrow my eyes at her. "Marshall spoke to me. Said you took time off, as you need a break. Was it a lie?"

"I wanted to surprise you."

I lean in close again so she can hear me over the bass. "You have. You're here with Lena."

She turns her head so only I hear the words with her lips close to my ear. "And you surprised me with that pretty girl in the bar."

I lean back and study her expression but it's damn hard to see past those made up eyes that are drawing me in.

"Are you coming home with me now?" I shouldn't need to ask but hell she has me rattled. When she gives a subtle nod I take her hand, and lead her toward the door.

wes

A s soon as we are out of the club I stop walking. "I've missed you." I kiss her. Show her how much with words failing me.

"I've missed you," she says quietly while avoiding my gaze.

I take her hand and wait while the concierge brings my car around to the front. "You needed a break? Did something happen I'm not aware of?"

"No. I'm tired and struggled during last night's gig."

I nod. "And when did you decide flying here was a good idea?"

"This morning."

"So being here with Lena wasn't premeditated. That wasn't part of the surprise?"

"No." She lowers her head.

"So how did you three meet up?"

Gar stares directly into my eyes. "I ran into Peta after seeing you in the bar with that girl." She holds up her hand and stops me from interrupting. "Glad I did. They distracted me long enough to work through my emotions."

The car pulls up and the concierge steps out leaving the car idling.

"Was your first thought to leave?" I ask as soon as her door closes.

"Yeah." She glances out the window and I refrain from responding hoping she'll keep talking. I don't care how much she says she needed a break, there's something she's hiding and I need her to open up. "It was awkward seeing *her* again. But then we slipped back into the nothing has changed mode. Only..." she shakes her head.

"What?"

"She hasn't changed. I didn't really want to be there but I chose to mend bridges, especially with Peta."

"You mean she hasn't changed being a fucking tapeworm." I grit my teeth. "She feeds off you, your success, your money—"

"Well, I wouldn't have been there if you weren't with someone else, so maybe I should be the one firing fucking accusations."

"She's a work colleague, nothing more."

"Who rubs your thigh and bats her lashes."

"Sounds like your jealous."

"I'm fucking tired that's what I am. I didn't want some bitch ruining my weekend. The old me woulda knocked her ass off the stool."

"The old you?" I grin.

"Still wanna give her a piece of my mind."

I lean over and rub her bare thigh. "Glad you didn't. And trust me you have nothing to worry about. So what do you want to do to revitalize?" I give a quick squeeze to her thigh. "What I have in mind means remaining in bed the entire day."

"You know me well," she whispers.

garnet

ntil now I avoided getting close to Wes in bright lights. I wasn't ready to explain the dressings on my face.

Lena's artwork concealed the evidence, and unless up close in good lighting it was barely noticeable. I stood on his right, tilted my face away.

Inside his apartment I keep my distance, as he flicks on lights and deactivates the security system. He strides to me, takes my face in his hands. When I angle my face away he stiffens feeling the material beneath his fingers.

I watch his expression falter.

"I tripped."

His gaze lands on mine. Holds it a moment. He nods then leads me to the bedroom.

His touch is oddly gentle, and considering we haven't fucked in weeks there's no urgency in his approach. Soft kisses. Slow hands. His caress is undoing me when I'm desperate to feel all of him to forget. I need to be fucked hard to extinguish everything else in my head.

Slowly, my dress is pried up and over my head.

"New?"

I shake my head. I don't want to say its Lena's and mention her name again. Probably mine really.

He stands back assessing me, and I watch his erection thicken against the band of his pants. I slide my thong down my thighs and reach for his buckle. "Use it if you think I've been a bad girl." I waggle my brow.

"Why would I think that?" His voice is hoarse.

"No reason." I kiss his bare chest. Lick my way down to his navel, as my fingers work the button and zip to free his cock. I take it in my hands, squeeze before my mouth finds the tip. I lick, caress, before closing my lips over the head and sliding along the length of him. Continuing with a steady rhythm until I hear his breath quicken, I speed up, my tongue increasing the suction to spur him on. His hands are tangled in my hair, guiding the rhythm. The moment before orgasm he cries out my name, thrusts into my mouth and I swallow quickly taking his load.

Pulling out, he steps out of his pants and lifts me onto his bed. Frantic kisses between my thighs, ready to repay the favor when his breathing normalizes. I open my legs wide, my back supported by pillows ready to indulge in pleasure.

It doesn't take much for me to climax with Wes' tongue and fingers working me equally.

Wes doesn't give me time to recover before he's hovering over me, his erection poking my clit. His cock slides in, and he stills watching my expression, thrusts slowly, gently, kissing my breasts, licking my nipples. His teeth pull gently on the rings and I buck in desire. The rhythm switches up and we build together. It's not enough to be loved tonight. I need more.

"Fuck me. I want you to fuck me," I whisper.

He stalls, stares so deep likes he's searching for my damn soul.

"Wes," I plead.

Then I'm flipped over, and onto my knees. He drives himself into me hard and fast, while hooking his hands under each thigh he lifts my legs higher and spreads my thighs wider. I'm exposed while he fucks me raw. I balance on my elbows while pain and pleasure course through me. I cry out multiple times as the orgasms blend, each hitting me with force one after the other. Wes thrusts hard, releasing my legs, groaning as he comes undone and collapses over me.

His weight stills any motion. Heavy breaths fill my ears. Pleasure still pulsing between my thighs.

Perfect.

garnet

"Fuck!"

My eyes flash open hearing Wes curse.

"What?" I croak out as I push up to my elbow. He remains quiet so I hit the side lamp. His hand is cupping his eye. "What happened?"

"Your elbow connected with my eye," he rasps.

"Shit." I lift his hand to take a look, strain to focus my vision in the bright light. His eye is closed and he squints to look at me. "I really am sorry—"

"You were talking in your sleep. More distressed. I reached over to calm you and you reacted like I was going to hurt you."

My lungs stop working. "What did I say?"

"I couldn't understand but you were groaning a lot."

"I was?"

"I didn't take you to be the kind to have nightmares."

"We all have nightmares," I say quickly. "Would you like me to grab an icepack?"

"I'd like you to be honest with me. Tell me what's really bothering you?"

"I needed a break." I shrug. "I thought you would be the one to understand."

"I am. I do. But nothing fits. This whole surprise thing. My gut is telling me there's more."

I nod. "There is. Can we talk about it in the morning?"

Wes rubs at his eye. "We can as long as there are no further hits to my face."

"There won't be." I curl up beside him and know I won't fall back into a deep sleep. My thoughts are directed to the dumb fuck and explaining my stupidity to Wes.

39

wes

The plane slows on the runway at LAX and my shoulders relax a little.

It's been four days.

Four days since she returned to LA, and to my house where the little fucker assaulted Gar. The wrenching pain in my gut has remained from the moment I saw the fine cuts to her cheek. She flinched as I removed the tape—not deep enough for sutures. For precaution I had my doctor come to the house and glue it, apply fresh dressings after she scrubbed the paint from her face. Stuck her with a tetanus shot and recommended she get tested for god knows what because who knows where that blade had been. She assured me her vaccinations were up to date. None of it reassured my erratic thoughts devising measures to protect her.

In the end, I won that argument. Safety measures are in place. I'm paying for her security guards, which she cursed every shocking word at me at the thought of someone following her around.

Gar didn't allow me to report the incident. I understood her reasons but it wasn't good enough in my eyes. She was adamant she wouldn't walk around alone. Well, Big Beau assured me no one will get past him when he's on her watch.

I check my watch as I head straight to Red Star to watch her gig. Then we'll have the remainder of the weekend together.

We need time to *make up* after the arguments last weekend. It was no surprise she fought me on *every* angle. Refused to be cowered into a corner by a creep. An incident she believes was a one-off.

"Just come here where I can goddamn look out for you," I had said to her.

"No. I'm not running." She had crossed her arms defiantly.

So now I'm here to negotiate a future, our future. All I know is I'm not prepared to lose her.

The club is pumping when the limo pulls up out front. I can hear the excitement before I enter the main door.

Gar is halfway through her performance. Her top is off as she canters the stage in her standard black bra and jeans.

The music takes a steady beat as she waves her hands in the air, connecting with the crowd. She fades the bass. Takes the mic and I assume she's going to sing. I make my way to the sidewall, to my usual post.

"Tonight I want to tell you a story…"

The crowd quiets for her.

"A dumb fuck attacked me the other night." She points to her cheek. "Cut my face."

Gasps echo from the crowd. Threats shouted for the attacker.

"I'm fine." She raises her hands to soothe the abuse. "But I want to talk to all of you about this. What to do if you're in a similar situation. Men and women are assaulted every day, I know this. So you need to fight back. Not be the victim. Make noise, get noticed." She points her hand to the crowd and to no one in particular. "He called me a skinny bitch and thought I'd be an easy target." She shakes her head, as though reliving the moment, and I want to stride up there and take her in my arms. "He had no respect. This bastard spoke to me like I was nothing. A piece of shit. And at first, I believed him. I was scared and caught off guard momentarily. Momentarily," she repeats louder. "I have a plan in my head about what to do in *these* situations. So to all of you out there, get a plan in case this ever happens to you!" She walks to the edge of the stage and kneels so she can look at faces in the crowd. "We need to be strong. We need to fight. We need to believe in ourselves and know we are not nothing. We are so much more," she yells the final words, and closes her hand into a fist. She pushes up and walks the length of the stage. "We need to find the love, not only for each other but for ourselves, and be ready if someone wants to take us down. We all need to empower each other." She stands and walks back to the deck. Turns the volume up and pumps the air.

Just when I think I know the beat it switches... and she *sings*. Sings about love, and the strength of her heart. I'm mesmerized watching her. Mesmerized listening to her. And something inside me awakens, acknowledges what she stands for. Gar cannot leave the city she loves, the people who flock to see her every weekend, call her their own. This is her home. She is doing what she's meant to do. And one of the lucky ones to be living a dream.

I dip my chin. This is how it is for now. But we'll remain together. I'll fight with every breath not to give up on us. Marshall might control my life now but it won't be forever.

She finishes and cups her hands in a heart and pulses it to the crowd. "I love you, and if this man steers me right..." she points to me, "... you might get to hear more tunes."

She smiles at me and the crowd erupts into applause.

I give her a nod, and reciprocate the smile.

"Yeah, you fucking like that!" she says to the crowd, and they scream louder.

I fucking love that.

Love her.

I push through the crowd. Security allows me to pass. I take the stairs to the stage two at a time. Pull her into my arms and spin her round, and round.

"This is how I feel since you came into my life," I shout over the cheering.

Gar wraps her arms and legs around me like a little monkey. "I love you, and want to be with you," she screams. "The fans deserve to know where my career might take me."

"Thank you. You don't have to leave all this,"
I confirm. "Just take it slow. One song at a time."
Then I kiss her for all her fans to see.

The End

ACKNOWLEDGEMENTS

To my author, and non-writing friends, thank you for supporting me on this journey. You were my cheerleaders who inspired me to finish the Spin Me Round series. I couldn't have done it without you.

To all the bloggers who supported me, a big thank-you, especially to Kim Sutton and Blogging For The Love Of Authors And Their Books! You're all amazing.

To my editors S.J. Thomas, and Kaylene Osborn at Swish Design and Editing, I am appreciative for all your help and expertise.

Kaylene you are remarkable and generous and I'm forever grateful to you!

A special thanks to Najla Qamber for the gorgeous cover.

And to you, the reader, a million thank-you's for buying my book. Most of all I hope you enjoyed it.

If you find the time, please leave a review on Goodreads and Amazon.

And please tell your friends, as there is nothing better than the word of mouth to spread good news. I love you all!